"What if what I really want is to stay married?"

It wasn't, but Jason was in a reckless mood after all his careful plans had unraveled in the course of an afternoon. One kiss wasn't enough to get him completely over the destruction this woman had caused. Plus, she'd piqued his curiosity about the divorce. Why was it so important to her? There were a lot of women who might find it convenient to be married to someone from a powerful fashion-industry family.

The fact that she didn't intrigued him.

Of course, Meredith had always been one of a kind.

Her genuine smile hit him in the not-yet-cooled lower half, further proving the point. No woman had ever turned him on with simply a grin. Except his wife, apparently.

* * *

Don't miss Meredith's sister's story, another Newlywed Games book, in *From Ex to Eternity*, also on sale this month from Harlequin Desire.

* * *

From Fake to Forever
is part of the Newlywed Games duet:
Two wedding dress designers finally get
their chance to walk down the aisle!

* * *

If you're on Twitter,
tell us what you think of Harlequin Desire!
#harlequindesire

Dear Reader,

It's raining weddings at Harlequin! If you read *From Ex to Eternity*, you've already met Cara's sister, Meredith, and likely hurried to pick up her story. She's an intriguing, unforgettable woman, as her Las Vegas weekend fling discovers when she shows up in his office two years later...along with the news that they're still married! Jason Lynhurst already has enough problems, and Meredith makes things worse. Or does she?

I loved twisting this marriage-of-convenience story—or rather, Meredith and Jason did it for me! They are two of the most headstrong characters I've ever had the pleasure of writing, and they took me along for the ride as Jason tried to keep their marriage platonic and Meredith tried to rekindle their love affair. All while Meredith infiltrated the world of New York fashion to complete the task Jason demanded in exchange for a divorce. It's a rush from beginning to end!

If you missed Cara and Keith's story, *From Ex to Eternity* is also available this month— pick it up today!

I hope you enjoy reading both sisters' stories as much as I enjoyed writing them.

Kat Cantrell

FROM FAKE
TO FOREVER

—

KAT CANTRELL

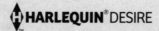

Recycling programs
for this product may
not exist in your area.

ISBN-13: 978-0-373-73383-5

From Fake to Forever

Copyright © 2015 by Kat Cantrell

All rights reserved. Except for use in any review, the reproduction or utilization of this work in whole or in part in any form by any electronic, mechanical or other means, now known or hereinafter invented, including xerography, photocopying and recording, or in any information storage or retrieval system, is forbidden without the written permission of the publisher, Harlequin Enterprises Limited, 225 Duncan Mill Road, Don Mills, Ontario M3B 3K9, Canada.

This is a work of fiction. Names, characters, places and incidents are either the product of the author's imagination or are used fictitiously, and any resemblance to actual persons, living or dead, business establishments, events or locales is entirely coincidental.

This edition published by arrangement with Harlequin Books S.A.

For questions and comments about the quality of this book, please contact us at CustomerService@Harlequin.com.

® and TM are trademarks of Harlequin Enterprises Limited or its corporate affiliates. Trademarks indicated with ® are registered in the United States Patent and Trademark Office, the Canadian Intellectual Property Office and in other countries.

Printed in U.S.A.

HARLEQUIN®
www.Harlequin.com

Kat Cantrell read her first Harlequin novel in third grade and has been scribbling in notebooks since she learned to spell. What else would she write but romance? She majored in literature, officially with the intent to teach, but somehow ended up buried in middle management in corporate America, until she became a stay-at-home mom and full-time writer.

Kat, her husband and their two boys live in north Texas. When she's not writing about characters on the journey to happily-ever-after, she can be found at a soccer game, watching the TV show *Friends* or listening to '80s music.

Kat was the 2011 Harlequin So You Think You Can Write winner and a 2012 RWA Golden Heart Award finalist for best unpublished series contemporary manuscript.

Books by Kat Cantrell

HARLEQUIN DESIRE

Marriage with Benefits
The Things She Says
The Baby Deal
Pregnant by Morning

Happily Ever After, Inc.

Matched to a Billionaire
Matched to a Prince

Newlywed Games

From Ex to Eternity
From Fake to Forever

Visit the Author Profile page at Harlequin.com for more titles.

One

Normally, a surprise trip to Manhattan ranked high on Meredith Chandler-Harris's list of Really Cool Things. A visit to one of the most highly respected fashion houses in the world hit the list even higher than that. Having to tell the man she'd spent two years trying to forget that they were married, not so much. It pretty much ruined Manhattan, fashion and—hell, even martinis.

That had been Jason's drink.

Meredith shifted as unobtrusively as possible on the leather couch as she waited for the receptionist to admit her to the inner sanctum of Jason Lynhurst, chief operating officer of Lyn Couture. Who was also Meredith's husband. Apparently.

"Mr. Lynhurst will see you now," the receptionist called in her frostiest voice.

Meredith always got frosty from women, who were largely unforgiving of the assets God had bestowed on her at birth. And she especially expected frosty from a woman who'd tried not-so-politely to show Meredith the door. She obviously had no clue who she was dealing with.

Lyn Couture bustled beyond the reception area, with sharply dressed men and women engaged in a myriad of tasks. Fascinated, Meredith craned her neck to peek at chalk outlines of sleek outfits stenciled on parchment and fabric swatches laid out on cluttered desks.

This was where the alchemy of fashion and style converged. It was enough to make a woman giddy. She adored everything about clothes: buying them, wearing them, owning them, matching them. But to a woman who wanted to buy half of her sister's wedding-dress-design company, Lyn Couture was so much more than a place of business—this was a mecca for like-minded people.

Even Meredith had a pair of Lyn jeans. Of course, she hadn't known who Jason was when she'd caught his eye across the dance floor at that club in Vegas. She'd only known that he moved like a man comfortable in his own body and had cheekbones to spare. And she'd wanted a piece of him. Only to learn two years later she'd bitten off a much bigger piece than she'd ever dreamed.

Curious gazes swung in Meredith's direction as she followed Frosty Receptionist to the corner office.

"Mr. Lynhurst?" the receptionist called through the open door. "Your visitor is here."

Mr. Lynhurst. Please. That man had done more wicked things to Meredith in one weekend than all the men since then…combined. Much to her chagrin. Wasn't there *one* who could make her forget the perfection of the man who had rocked her world so very long ago?

"Thanks, hon. I'll take it from here." Meredith skirted the receptionist and swept into the office as if she owned it because that's how you got people's attention.

And she needed Jason's attention. Because she had to talk him into a quiet divorce. Immediately. It was the only way she'd be able to stomach approaching her father about a loan so she could buy into her sister's business.

Plus, she wasn't ready to be married, to Jason or anyone. Not until she figured out who she was going to be when she grew up. That was why in the cold light of morning, the Las Vegas-style marriage ceremony from the night before had seemed like the opposite of a good idea. The paperwork was never supposed to be filed, but here she was. Married to Jason.

The man in question sat behind a glass desk, modern and sharp. Much like the man. As their gazes collided... and held...her breath stuttered. Oh, yeah. *That* was why no man in existence could erase Jason from her mind.

Those cheekbones. To die for. Artfully messed-up spiky pale blond hair, begging for her fingers to slide through it as she pulled him down for a scorching kiss. Witty, sensual and, God Almighty, he *listened* when she talked. Men rarely glanced above Meredith's shoulders, but Jason had asked her opinions, accepted her thoughts.

He was the man she'd compared to all other men and found them lacking. And two years hadn't diminished his potency in the slightest.

Jason rose from behind his desk, mouthwatering in a slim dark suit likely conceived, created and cut yards from his office.

"Meredith. You look well." If she'd surprised him with this unexpected visit, he kept it from his smooth voice.

"Thanks for seeing me on short notice." Well, wasn't this pleasant? Two people reacquainting themselves, who'd never thought they'd lay eyes on each other again. No point in beating around the bush. "We have a problem. The more quickly and quietly we can resolve it, the better."

A shield snapped over his expression. "I sincerely hope you are not about to tell me you got pregnant and are just now getting around to mentioning it to me."

What kind of woman did he take her for? She tamped back the ire. They really didn't know each other very well. Their wild weekend in Vegas had been about being at a crossroads, not about finding a lifelong mate.

The marriage had been a mistake. They both knew that.

"No, nothing like that." Meredith waved it off and perched on the edge of one of the chairs flanking Jason's desk, hoping he'd take the hint and sit back down. This was a friendly visit.

He relaxed, slightly, but didn't sit down. "Then anything else is manageable. What can I do for you?"

This was so weird. She'd spent hours upon hours sliding her slick body against this man's. Her tongue had tasted every inch of the skin hiding under that suit. They were strangers, then and now. And yet, not strangers. It felt oddly like they'd seen each other only yesterday.

"So, funny story." She grinned as if it really was. "Remember how we found that all-night marriage-license place and then thought it would be so great to tie the knot in Vegas to seal the Grown-Up Pact?"

The Grown-Up Pact.

It had seemed brilliant at the time…after four rounds of tequila shots and countless cosmopolitans and martinis. After that first initial meeting of gazes, they hadn't left each other's company the rest of the weekend. They'd embarked on a seemingly endless conversation during which Meredith spilled more of her soul to this man she'd just met than she ever had to anyone else. And he'd claimed the same. They'd both been searching for something, anything, to help them navigate the bridge between the caprices of youth and the rest of their lives.

The Grown-Up Pact had never been about staying married, but about proving they could do grown-up things, that a commitment like marriage wasn't so scary if they could do it together.

Ironic how the marriage that was supposed to prove they were grown-ups had resulted in a very adult problem.

"Of course I remember," he said. "It was the only time I've ever acted on a stupid idea."

She sighed. That made one of them. She did stupid things all the time. The Grown-Up Pact should have given her the fortitude to move past her beauty-pageant pedigree and find a place in the world where she could be appreciated for what went on between her temples. But she hadn't found that place, not yet.

"Turns out the marriage license got filed somehow."

"What?" Jason's expression turned flinty. "How did that happen? You were supposed to shred the license."

"I did! Well, I threw it away." She *had* to have thrown it away. The problem was she couldn't precisely recall the actual throwing away part. "No one said anything about shredding."

"That's what you do with something you don't want to fall into the wrong hands, Meredith." That seemed to be enough to get him to finally sit down. "Credit card numbers, legal documents. Marriage licenses that you realize the next morning you never should have registered for in the first place."

He threaded fingers through his messy hair and her own fingers flexed in response, aching to feel him again. It was a brutal reminder that she'd half thought they might catch up for old times' sake, once they sorted out this stupid mistake she'd made. One last roll in Jason's bed would probably cure her for good and then she could finally move on.

The fierce expression on his face didn't exactly put a warm fuzzy in her tummy.

"So, it happened," she said. "We're legally married and have been for two years. Now we need to deal with it. And then maybe we can, you know, have a drink or two later?"

The suggestion wasn't at all subtle, but no one did brazen better. She had a perverse need to see if any of the spark between them still existed.

"Deal with it? Oh, I see. You're here because you saw the announcement of my engagement and you want a payoff." He nodded wearily. "How much do you want?"

Jason was engaged? That was great. Obviously he'd want to handle this quickly and quietly, as well. She kept trying to convince herself of the greatness and failed.

The disappointment at learning he'd moved on so much

better than she had was bitter and sharp. There would be no catching up, then. No last wild weekend.

"I don't want your money, Jason. Just a no-fault, no-division-of-assets divorce."

"Sure." His sarcasm was thick. "As soon as you found out I was Bettina Lynhurst's son back in Vegas, little dollar signs must have danced before your eyes. Admit it. You filed the marriage license on purpose, hoping to cash in later. Frankly, I'm shocked it took this long for your trick to play out."

Her mouth fell open. "You've obviously forgotten I'm a Chandler *and* a Harris. I don't need your piddly fashion-empire fortune. My father's money built Houston. So keep your snotty dollar signs, sign the divorce papers and go about your business."

Of course, she'd cut up all her father's credit cards, but Jason didn't need to know that.

For God knew what reason, Jason grinned. The tension leeched away as he sat back in his chair. "I wish I could say I'd forgotten how sassy you are. If you're not here for money, what are you here for?"

"Is this rocket science?" Airily, she motioned to him so it would seem like something other than the really big deal it actually was. Her family could *not* find out she hadn't taken care of this problem. "It's in both our interests to get a quiet divorce. So I'm here to get that done."

"You already have papers drawn up? Great. Give me a copy and I'll shoot them to my lawyer. As long as everything's in order, I'll sign and mail you a copy. Thanks for coming by. I'll walk you out."

He stood. She didn't. "What guarantee do I have that you won't spill all of this to the media?"

If her father found out how supremely rash his daughter had acted, he'd never agree to give her a loan to buy half of Cara's design business. And Meredith wanted to prove once and for all she had what it took to make something of herself.

This loan was the key to the rest of Meredith's life. Finally, she'd be able to call herself something other than a pageant winner. Finally, other people would have something to call her besides a former Miss Texas: a grown-up.

Jason's laughter was harsh. "Why in the world would I want to advertise something so ridiculous as a spontaneous wedding in Las Vegas to a woman I'd just met who's boneheaded enough to accidentally file the marriage license?"

"Well, don't hold back, sweetie. Tell me how you really feel." She eyed him. "We're on the same page. I'd prefer no one found out I married someone boneheaded enough to have me. Here's a copy of the papers."

"I'll have my lawyer check them out. Don't go anywhere," he advised. "I want to settle this before you leave town."

"I'll be around for a few days, but no longer, so make it snappy."

With a flourish, she wrote the name of her hotel and her cell-phone number on a sticky note and pasted it to his lapel in a senseless effort to touch him one last time.

Shame about that fiancée. More was the shame that Jason Lynhurst was totally over Meredith.

But the biggest shame was that she couldn't say the same.

Meredith. Of all the freaking people to waltz into Jason's office on an otherwise unremarkable Friday.

She was the only woman who'd ever enticed him out from behind his all-business exterior, the only woman who could claim she'd slept in his bed, when normally, he kept women away from his personal space. Their brief relationship had been crazy, wild, the stuff of his hottest fantasies—and totally out of character.

Meredith was also the only woman he'd ever considered

truly dangerous. For his well-being, his future, his state of mind. And definitely dangerous to his self-control. Because he couldn't resist her back in Vegas and he had a feeling nothing had changed.

This was not the time, nor the place, to dwell on that.

He had a meeting with Avery in fifteen minutes and his sister was going to lord it over him for being late. And getting across town at this hour was more impossible than wishing himself invisible. Hefting his messenger bag to his other shoulder, Jason hailed a taxi instead of taking the company car because it would take too long to retrieve it from the garage.

Yet another disruption in his jam-packed day, thanks to that blast from the past.

Once Jason slid into the cab, his mind immediately flipped back to the bombshell Meredith had dropped on him. Apparently he couldn't resist thinking about her any more than he could resist that come-hither look she'd used so effectively in Vegas to drive him just this side of insane.

Married. To Meredith.

Once, it had seemed like a fantastic plan, to bond himself—symbolically, of course, as part of the Grown-Up Pact—to a woman who seemed to effortlessly understand his misery and pain and then take it all away.

Their brief affair had its place. In the history books.

Vegas had been a spontaneous trip, born out of his confusion and frustration over his parents' announcement. Not only were they divorcing after thirty years of marriage, but they were also splitting apart Lynhurst Enterprises, the company they'd founded. Lyn Couture to Bettina, Hurst House Fashion to Paul. Jason would stay at Lyn and Avery would go to Hurst House. Everyone seemed fine with it—except no one asked Jason's opinion.

He hated it. The legacy he'd been born to, depended on, planned for, was gone. Fractured beyond repair. All at once, he couldn't deal with it and jetted off to forget in Vegas.

Meredith had been a balm to his broken soul. Exactly what he'd needed at the time, and she'd honed his focus. If it hadn't been for the turmoil going on at home, he'd never have been open to what she'd offered, but thank God he'd decided to play by different rules for one weekend. He'd left her in that hotel room with a kiss and a thank-you and flown back to New York with new purpose.

He'd reunite Lynhurst Enterprises under one umbrella again or die trying.

That was what he'd hoped to gain with the Grown-Up Pact. A direction, a sense that he could take on this new paradigm and succeed. And the seed of his plan was about to bear fruit.

This meeting with Avery was the next step. Lyn belonged with Hurst House and Jason belonged at the helm as the CEO of the newly repaired company. At least in this, he and Avery agreed and they'd put their animosity aside to work toward it in secret. Today, they'd start putting their takeover plan into action.

Because he couldn't help himself, Jason did an internet search on his phone for the Clark County, Nevada, marriage registrar, and sure enough, a quick search revealed the plain-text record of his very legal marriage to Meredith Lizette Chandler-Harris.

A blip in judgment, one he couldn't imagine explaining to the people in his real life. That's why they'd tracked down the officiant who'd performed the ceremony and asked for the license back so it couldn't be filed. So what had happened? Jason called his lawyer to let him figure it out and jumped from the cab at the coffeehouse Avery had selected for their clandestine takeover bid, which was near her pretentious Tribeca loft.

As expected, his sister waited, not so patiently, at the back booth. Drumming her fingers in annoyance, she glared at Jason all the way across the room.

"Where have you been? I'm meeting with the *Project*

Runway advertising people in an hour." Avery's snootiness was in full force today. "Not all of us got a cushy position at Lyn doing Mother's bidding twenty-four seven. I have an actual job to do."

"Hello to you, too," he responded mildly. Avery liked nothing more than to rile him, so he never indulged her. "Since you're so busy, you should have picked a place closer to Midtown."

Jason pulled the paperwork from his bag, which detailed the restructuring of Lyn Couture and Hurst House Fashion back into one company, and set the document on the wooden tabletop. This had been his contribution, while Avery had managed the branding and design aspects, as they hoped to launch the re-formed company with a new spring line. The publicity would be great for all their labels. She also planned to give notice at Hurst House and take a job at Lyn in an effort to make a merger more attractive.

Avery glanced at the sheaf of papers he'd slaved over for weeks. Then she did a double take and raised her brows. "This says you're going to be the CEO. Except you aren't. I am."

"Are you insane? Why do you think I've been so passionate about this—so I can work for you instead of Mom?" Avery was delusional. She couldn't handle a CEO position and besides, it was his. He'd gone to Harvard to get a business degree in anticipation of it. "I'll take care of you, don't worry."

She tossed her long blond hair. "Why do you think *I've* been working on this? Lynhurst Enterprises is mine."

"Like hell." Avery had come to hate the split and wanted Lynhurst reunited as much as he did or he'd never have agreed to work with her. Why hadn't he seen that she'd also developed an appetite for power?

"I'm the oldest—it's a given that I'll take over the company once we get it back the way it was."

"It's not a given," Jason countered fiercely and lowered

his voice. "I've worked harder and longer than anyone, including you."

His entire life had been groomed toward the concept of stepping into his father's shoes as the head of Lynhurst. Avery and Bettina had critical roles on the design and marketing side, of course, but they weren't visionaries. They couldn't keep a huge ship like Lynhurst afloat *and* steer it in the right direction, especially not after merging the two halves. It took more than a good eye for color to manage a business.

"That's a complete lie." She flicked manicured fingers at Jason's face, a crafty smile playing about her thin lips. "Whose idea was it to tackle this puppy together? Not yours. It has more punch if we're united and take this proposal to Mom and Dad as fait accompli. Without that, you'd have nothing. Tell me you didn't think I was going to hand over the top spot to you, little brother."

A deliberate jab, like birth order meant something in the grand scheme of things.

"There's no 'handing over' of anything. I've earned that position with these merger plans, not to mention what I've accomplished as COO of Lyn Couture." Hell, he'd earned the CEO position with his coup of an engagement to Meiling Lim alone.

His fiancée's father owned the largest textile business in Asia, and Jason's marriage to Meiling would solidify the partnership between Lyn Couture and overseas manufacturing houses. It was a match negotiated over the boardroom table and made excellent business sense.

Meiling's delicate features and proper demeanor represented exactly the kind of wife an up-and-coming CEO needed. They liked each other and had similar goals for their union, namely, that it would benefit their families. Neither of them expected a love match and, in fact, they both preferred this sort of arrangement. He would gladly include her in his life and they'd have a calm, advantageous marriage…unlike the tumultuous, frenzied, crazy-making one he'd have with someone like Meredith.

The last thing he needed was a woman in his life who goaded him into making bad decisions. He'd leave that kind of woman to his father.

Jason was incredibly fortunate Meiling's traditional family seemed forward-thinking enough to overlook his Western heritage. He was a man navigating a world largely populated by women. He needed an edge. Meiling was it. Nothing could stop his careful plans.

Except for Avery's misguided notion of slipping CEO out from under him. Which would happen when camels learned to swim.

"Why don't we worry about who will be the boss when the merger is done?" Jason suggested smoothly.

They needed to focus on more important things or there wouldn't be a CEO position to fill. Bettina and Paul were very comfortable in their current roles as CEOs of their halves, especially Bettina since she largely depended on Jason to advise her, but the winds of change were upon his parents whether they liked it or not.

Avery scowled but nodded. "Fine. For now. But don't think you're getting away with something. I'm not going to back off. Let's get to work."

They hashed out details for the next twenty minutes until his sister had to jet to her *Project Runway* meeting. In the cab back to Lyn, Jason dialed Meiling. It was only appropriate she hear about the marriage-license snafu from him. Hopefully she would appreciate the expedience of already having divorce papers in hand. Once his lawyer looked over them, it would be a done deal and he'd never have to see Meredith again…except in his mind where her luminous eyes beckoned him into an upside-down world where pleasure and understanding and connection didn't seem like such foreign concepts.

He had to stop thinking about her. It was disrespectful to Meiling, if nothing else. There was no scenario in which Meredith being in his life—even briefly—made a bit of sense.

Two

It was past seven o'clock, but Meredith's stomach seemed stuck on Central Standard Time and dinner had about the same appeal as a tetanus shot. *Nerves.* Everything rode on this very quiet, very quick divorce.

Lars, her father's lawyer, had been so patient when he'd explained that he'd found the marriage record during a thorough investigation of her father's beneficiaries. If her father hadn't decided to update his will, she might never have known the marriage to Jason existed and thankfully, it had come out *before* she approached her father about the loan.

Without a prenuptial agreement, Jason could claim to be a beneficiary to her father's billions if he chose to fight for them in court. Thank God Lars had been her father's lawyer since before she was born and was sweet on her. He'd agreed to keep her stupidity a secret until she took care of the divorce and then he'd advised her to come clean to her father or he would be forced to mention it on her behalf.

A legal marriage she didn't know about smacked of carelessness, and she couldn't stand the thought of asking her father for a loan in the same breath as admitting a mistake she hadn't yet fixed. Her sister, Cara, would never do something rash like a quickie Vegas wedding to a man she'd just met, let alone mess up the undoing of it. Meredith wanted to prove she could be as responsible as Cara. Once Meredith had Jason's signature, she could present the marriage and divorce as a package deal, and hopefully everyone would agree she'd handled it like an adult who deserved a loan and a partnership opportunity in a successful business.

Good thing Meredith wasn't hungry. If one of the trendy restaurants around her hotel tried to swipe her credit card to pay for the exorbitant menu prices, the plastic would probably catch fire and disintegrate. The credit limit on her Visa was laughable, but she'd qualified for it all by herself. No one could take away the satisfaction of paying her own way—that was what the Grown-Up Pact should have helped her realize, but it had taken a lot longer for the epiphany than she'd expected.

She hadn't counted on sticking around this expensive Manhattan hotel over the weekend, but she recognized Jason's wisdom in being available, just in case.

No biggie. She probably didn't need to eat anyway. Better to get used to lean times now because once she bought into Cara's business, she'd have a loan to repay on top of a paltry savings account.

Listlessly, she ran through the TV channels a fourth time. When her cell phone beeped, she greedily grabbed it in hopes of taking her mind off Jason.

Except it was a text from the man himself: I'm in the lobby. Text me your room number.

A quick, sharp thrill shot through her midsection. Oh, she didn't fool herself for a minute. He wasn't here to take her up on the ill-advised invitation for a drink. The man was engaged and she sincerely hoped he wasn't the kind of guy who'd fool around on his fiancée. If he *was* interested in "catching up," she wasn't—poaching on men in committed relationships wasn't her style.

She texted him back and hightailed it to the bathroom to splash on some perfume and freshen her makeup because Chandler-Harris women did not allow anyone to see their cracks.

The knock startled her despite her expecting it. *That was fast.*

She opened the door and the dark expression on Jason's face swept out to engulf her and not in a good way. The back of her neck crawled. "What's wrong?"

"Just let me in. I'm not having this conversation with you while lounging in the hall."

Silently, she pushed the door wide, forcing him to slide past her to enter the room. It was a deliberate ploy, but his solid body brushed hers deliciously and she wasn't sorry she'd done it.

Jason filled the hotel room and she couldn't tear her gaze from him. "I take it you aren't planning to ask me to dinner. Which would be totally fine, by the way. I haven't eaten yet."

"You've ruined everything," he said shortly. "Everything. I've worked so blasted hard for two years, and in one afternoon, it's gone. Poof."

"What are you talking about? I'm here to *fix* the problem."

"I told my fiancée the cute story of a torrid weekend in Vegas and how, get this, it's so funny, but it turns out I'm still married. She was not amused. In fact, she was so unamused, our engagement is over."

"Oh, Jason! I'm so sorry." Meredith's hand flew to her mouth involuntarily. How terrible. He had to be beside himself. No wonder his mood seemed so black. "I never imagined—"

"So here's how this is going to go. You cost me a very important contact in the textile industry. You owe me. And you are going to pay, starting right now."

She took a step backward as his ire rolled over her. "Uh, pay how?"

This was not the man she remembered from Vegas. He looked the same, had the same rocking body and a voice that should be required by law to talk dirty to her twenty-four seven. But this Jason Lynhurst was harder, more brittle. She didn't like it.

"In as many unpleasant ways as I can devise," he muttered and swept her with a look. "But not *that* way. This is strictly business, sweetheart. I need you to do something for me."

Since he'd just lost his fiancée, and likely was nursing a broken heart, she'd let the condescension slide. "I'm truly sorry that your fiancée is upset. I'm sure you can smooth things over. Do that thing with your mouth, you kno—"

"Meiling is not upset."

Fire flared from his gaze, giving her a great big clue who the upset party was in this equation. Since he'd interrupted her again, she crossed her arms and perched on the desk so he could burn off that mad.

"If she's not upset, what is she?"

Jason started pacing, rearranging his spiky hair with absent fingers as he stomped around in her small room, shedding his suit jacket as he went.

"She's unwilling to associate with someone who would marry a stranger in a crass Vegas wedding and then fail to follow up to ensure the marriage was dissolved. Her exact words." He tossed his jacket on the bed with a great deal more force than necessary. "I've embarrassed her in front of her family, and in her world, that's unforgivable. So there's no smoothing it over."

The light dawned. "You weren't in love with her."

Why that made her so happy, she couldn't pinpoint. But the realization moved through her with a wicked thrill nonetheless.

Jason shot her an annoyed glare. "Of course not. It was a business arrangement, and now I've lost the in I had into the Asian textile market. Lyn needed Meiling's connections. Since this is all your fault, you owe me."

Okay, this was not what she'd anticipated. Where was the sensitive, passionate man she'd spent many luscious hours with once upon a time? He'd been replaced with a coldhearted suit who possessed not a shred of romance in his soul.

"My fault?" She tightened her crossed arms before she used one to right-hook him to the ground. "Seems like your fiancée—sorry, ex-fiancée—called it exactly right. You didn't follow up, either. Actually, you should be thanking me that I came to you with the truth before you got married. You'd be guilty of bigamy. Imagine explaining *that* to your Meiling."

"I depended on you to destroy the papers." He made a noise of disgust. "I shouldn't have, obviously."

That stung. Mostly because the implication—that she couldn't be counted on and wasn't smart enough to handle a simple task—was actually true in this case. "You're not endearing me to your cause, honey. Doesn't seem like I owe you anything but an apology. Which I've already given."

"You want to play hardball?" He advanced on her, the look in his eyes enigmatic and edgy. "Fine. I can indulge you. I lost an advantage and you're going to help me regain it. Granted, you don't have Meiling's connections, but I'm sure you've got many tricks up your sleeve. Until I get back on track, what's my hurry to sign the divorce papers?"

He stopped not a foot from her as his meaning sank in. He wasn't going to give her the divorce unless she did whatever it was that he wanted. Which still hadn't been clearly established.

Poking a finger in the center of his chest, she held her ground. "You wouldn't dare."

"Try me. I've got nothing to lose."

Gazes deadlocked, they stared at each other. No way would she blink first. Or move her index finger from his hard torso.

God in Heaven, that beautiful face of his. She soaked

it in and something sharp tore right through her abdomen. Many a morning over the past two years, she'd woken in a cold sweat with no idea what she'd dreamed, but certain Jason Lynhurst had played a starring role in it. That face lingered in her mind's eye far past the time when she should have forgotten it.

And here he was. Her fingers relaxed and flattened against his chest, easily, as if her palm belonged there. He glanced down and back up, meeting her gaze again with lowered lids. As if the thrumming tension had wound through him with equal fervor.

"If you've got nothing to lose, then I'd be more than happy to try you," she murmured.

She bunched his shirt in her fist and reeled him in. He hesitated for an eternity and then their lips met. The sweet taste of Jason swept through her and it was as if they'd never been apart. She nearly wept as Jason's arms came around her, drawing her closer.

This was the Jason of Vegas, the one she'd worked so hard to forget and couldn't.

Oh, yes. Her heart burst into motion, pumping euphoria through her veins as if it hadn't beaten in two long years. Hungrily, he sucked her deeper into the kiss and sparks danced behind her eyelids.

She pulled back, chest heaving from the effort of not diving into him with abandon. As they stared at each other, locked in a long moment, a glimpse of the man he'd been flitted through his features.

Something pulled at her heart. Oh, that was not good. *That* was why she'd never forgotten him—he'd taken a piece of her she'd never meant to give.

"Now that we've gotten that out of the way, can we start over?" she asked, her voice more tremulous than she would have liked.

Because she'd just realized letting him go in Vegas might have been the biggest mistake of her life.

* * *

In spite of it all, a chuckle spilled from Jason's mouth and reluctantly, he let his arms drop from the siren he'd somehow wound up kissing. He'd come here to wring her neck, but instead, she'd expertly defused his mood.

But that didn't mean they'd be falling right back into a crazy-town affair, not when so much was at stake. Not when he couldn't seem to keep his hands off her. "Depends on what the definition of starting over is."

Meredith pursed her kiss-stung lips, and he decided it was better to put a little more distance between them. She was even more dangerous than he'd realized and he refused to follow in his father's footsteps. Paul had left Bettina for a younger, sexier wife, with no regard to the consequences to his company or his family. Obviously, it was in the Lynhurst blood to let passion rule, but that didn't have to be Jason's fate and *someone* had to step up where his father had failed.

Jason had a vision for putting the pieces of his life back together and no woman would sway him from realizing it. He was stronger than his father.

While he flopped into one of the overstuffed chairs in the sitting area of her hotel room, she crossed to the minibar and pulled two beers from the fridge, flipped off the caps expertly and handed him one.

"I don't want to be at odds, Jason. You're upset. I get that. But don't come in here slinging ultimatums and expect me to fall in line. Let's do this differently."

What the hell. He loosened his tie, guzzled a third of the cold dark beer and raised his eyebrows. "Which is how?"

She took the opposite chair and swung it around to face him, settling into it with her beer. Kicking off her heels, she curled her feet under her and propped her chin on her hand. "Talk to me. Like you used to. Tell me what you want in exchange for the divorce. I might volunteer to give it to you, for old times' sake."

Like you used to. As if they had history.

But really, didn't they? Just because it had only been one weekend didn't make it any less significant, whether he'd like to go back in time and erase it or not.

"What if what I really want is to stay married?"

It wasn't, but he was in a reckless mood after all his careful plans had unraveled in the course of an afternoon. One kiss wasn't enough to get him completely over the destruction this woman had caused. Plus, she'd piqued his curiosity about the divorce. Why was it so important to her? There were a lot of women who might find it convenient to be married to someone from a powerful fashion-industry family. The fact that she didn't intrigued him.

Of course, Meredith had always been one of a kind.

Her genuine smile hit him in the not-yet-cooled lower half, further proving the point. No woman had ever turned him on with simply a grin. Except his wife, apparently.

"You don't want to stay married any more than I do," she said. "The fact that you're threatening me with it tells me you need something very badly. What?"

His return smile shouldn't have been so easy, but her mind had always been the most attractive thing about her. He might never have left Vegas with a solid idea of how to heal the fractures in his life without her influence. Why not continue the trend?

"Do you remember why I was in Vegas?"

"I remember everything, including that cute birthmark on your butt. Your parents divorced and split up Lynhurst. You were a wreck over it." She waggled her brows. "Or you were until I distracted you."

It had happened two years ago. The memories shouldn't be so sharp, but they were…for both of them, obviously. "You did take care of me, quite well. And vice versa, if I recall."

"Oh, yeah. That was never in question." She shut her

eyes for a beat and hummed happily under her breath. "Best nineteen orgasms of my life."

"You kept track?"

She glanced at him from under lowered lashes, her gaze hot and full of appreciation. "Darling, I didn't have to keep track. Every one of them is burned into my center. Indelibly."

He let himself drown in memories of her for a moment. None of the barriers he easily employed with other women seemed to have an effect on her anyway. "Yeah. I can see your point."

The experience was scored across his soul, as well. Meredith had brought out a wild side he hadn't even realized existed. Or maybe it only existed because of her, which was all the more reason to stay far away.

"Was there a reason you brought that up?" Meredith asked. "We seem to be stuck on it, when I could have sworn you had something else entirely you wanted to chat about."

He shook his gaze free from the seductive depths of Meredith's gaze and cleared his throat.

Obviously, he needed to take a cold shower if he hoped to accomplish anything. Whatever power she held over him couldn't be allowed to interfere with the endgame. "I spent the last two years executing the plan I came up with in Vegas. It's simple. Reunite Lyn Couture and Hurst House under the Lynhurst Enterprises umbrella and step into the CEO position. Who better to run it than me, right?"

Slinging a shapely leg over the arm of the chair, she tossed back the last of her beer as her skirt rode up to reveal a healthy slice of gorgeous thigh. "Yep. You've got CEO written all over you."

"Meiling was a part of that plan." *A critical part.* She was the kind of wife a CEO needed, not the overblown sex goddess in the opposite chair. But he had to work with what he had. "Now that she's out of the picture, I have to come up with plan B."

"That's where I come in."

He nodded, relieved for some odd reason that she still read him so well. "I don't want to use the divorce as leverage."

"But you will."

Transparency meant she saw the not-so-nice-guy parts, as well, and that made him a little uncomfortable. He shrugged. "This is my legacy. I cannot fathom veering from the course I've laid out and that means I have to improvise if I want to fix the rift in my family's company. You fill the gap where Meiling's advantage used to be and I'll sign the divorce papers."

Meredith was a loose cannon—prone to dropping projectiles wherever she went. But she had a sharp wit and determination and best of all, she wanted something from him. That was the best combination possible under the circumstances.

"Why don't you sign them now and I'll offer to help as a thank-you?" she countered sweetly and that was the opening he'd been waiting for.

He cocked his head. "Why are you so hot for a divorce from a guy you didn't even know you were married to last week? Am I such a bad catch?"

Her giggle warmed his insides. A lot. Too much.

"I have never thought of you as a fish."

Which didn't answer the question at all. He should sign the papers right now and let her go back to Houston. But he couldn't, and he really didn't want to examine why it was so important that Meredith help him because he suspected it had too much to do with this nameless draw between them.

And that was a problem. One of many.

But he did need an edge; that much was still true.

If Avery would only drop her bid for CEO, he wouldn't have to play this game of chicken with Meredith. But Avery would definitely dig in her heels and she was a Lynhurst—that made her a treacherous opponent. He didn't for a minute underestimate his sister's vindictiveness or her strategic mind. He'd let her have the CEO position over his dead body. Meredith was his secret advantage and she owed him.

Now he had to figure out how she could help.

"This goes both ways, you know." He flipped a hand between them. "I'm talking. You have to talk, too. Tell me why this divorce is so important."

She sighed and her expression blanked. It was wrong on her. Normally, her beautiful face glowed with expressiveness and he was a little sorry he'd brought up the question. But not entirely. She'd been trying to weasel out of spilling this information for too long.

"You have a dream and so do I," she said and it was clear she was choosing her words carefully. "I've been advised that in order to pursue mine, it would be beneficial to have my affairs in order. Correction—affair. I have no interest in being married. To you, or anyone. So sign the papers and everyone wins."

Now he was thoroughly intrigued, especially because he'd never in a million years label the reuniting of Lynhurst as a dream. It was a fact. "What's your dream, Meredith? Tell me."

"Why?" she asked suspiciously. "More leverage?"

Oh, yeah, she was no dummy. And that turned him on as much as everything else in her full package. More maybe. The fact that she was so savvy about his motivation changed it instantly. "No, because I'm curious. My mouth has been between your legs. That gives me special rights to know what's between your ears, too."

Her long, slow smile blew the blank expression away. Better. And worse.

"You win. But only because that's a great point and I happen to like it." She retrieved another beer and handed him a second, as well, then settled into her chair.

He tapped the longneck. "Trying to get me drunk so you can take advantage of me?"

She snorted. "Honey, I don't need alcohol for that."

Unfortunately, she might be right. All the more reason to nail down an agreement about their future interaction—which would be minimal. "So I made a great point. You liked it. Spill your beans."

"I'm buying into my sister's wedding-dress business." And then she clammed up with a show of drinking her beer.

There was more. He could sense it beneath the surface. "Seems like being married might be a bonus for that line of work."

"It's not, okay? Not this way." She shook her head. "I can't tell my family I did tequila shots in Vegas and wound up married to some guy. They'd never take me seriously again."

As he thoroughly and uniquely understood the sentiment, he grinned. "You make it sound tawdry. You can't tell them we fell in love?"

"Please. You can't even say that with a straight face and neither could I. They'd wonder why we haven't had any contact in two years, for one thing."

"Now that you mention it, I'm curious. Did you ever think about looking me up?"

He had briefly entertained the idea of contacting her on the plane home but then dismissed it as he hashed through mental plans about what it would take to get Lynhurst Enterprises back together. Besides, no one could be involved with Meredith long-term; the idea was ludicrous. She wasn't the kind of woman you settled down with. She was too lush, too distracting, too…everything. She'd compelled him to make stupid decisions without even opening her mouth.

He'd known then she'd spell disaster for his plans. Regrettably, he'd underestimated how catastrophic she'd ultimately be.

"Not once." Casually, she lifted the beer to her lips. Too casually, and he saw the guilt in the depths of her eyes. But why she'd lie was a mystery. "We agreed to part ways in Vegas. The Grown-Up Pact wasn't about actually staying married, right? It was about proving we could take grown-up steps. If we could do it together, we could do it apart. So why stonewall me on this divorce? Makes no sense."

"Does, too. Getting married had value. Staying married has advantages, too."

"For you. Though I have yet to hear how."

The time had come to lay it all on the line. "In order to reunite Lynhurst Enterprises, I have to take a strategic plan to the executive committees of Lyn Couture and Hurst House Fashion. My former fiancée's father owns the largest textile company in Asia and our marriage would have solidified a partnership with Lyn Couture, thus lowering production costs dramatically. Hurst House would want to benefit from this association and from my leadership."

Meredith could never fill that gap, but there had to be some way to spin this situation to his advantage.

"My sister, Avery," he continued, "was the second half of the plan. She runs the branding and marketing for Hurst House and we planned for her to quit Hurst House to come work for Lyn. Without her, the company would flounder, thus forcing my father, the current CEO of Hurst, to consider merging."

There was more, much more, but he kept those cards close to the vest. She didn't need to know his entire strategy.

"That's quite brilliant." Genuine appreciation shone from Meredith's gaze. "Sorry a weekend in Vegas a million years ago messed it all up."

The weekend in Vegas had helped him conceive this plan. Without it, he might never have come up with it. Ironic that the same weekend had come back to bite him.

"There's more. Avery's not on board with the plan anymore. She wants the CEO spot and I wouldn't put it past her to cook up her own scheme." Instantly, he knew how Meredith could provide that missing advantage. "I need someone she doesn't know to be my spy at Hurst House. Someone firmly on my side who can tell me what she's up to."

Meredith lit up but then quickly tamped back her excitement. "You want me to be a *spy* in a New York fashion house? In exchange for a divorce? That doesn't seem like a fair trade."

"Really?" Nonchalantly, he swallowed the last of his beer. "What would?"

A crafty glint in her eye raised the hair on the back of his neck.

"You have to put me on the payroll."

That's what she wanted? He'd expected her to ask for full marriage benefits, which would have been very difficult to refuse. Though he would have refused, for the sake of Lynhurst. He couldn't afford to let a woman cloud his vision. "Sure. I have no problem compensating you, though you'd have to be on the payroll at Hurst so no one suspects anything. What else?"

"The marriage stays a secret, now and after the divorce is final. I can't let it become known or my wedding-dress dream is over."

"That's easy. I don't care for anyone to know about it, either."

If Avery got ahold of that bit of information, she'd use it to her advantage somehow. The last thing Jason needed was to give someone leverage—someone other than him, that was.

She eyed him. "That's not what it sounded like a minute ago. You were all set to blab to your family about how we were in love."

"I was kidding. Love might make the world go round, but it tears businesses apart." Like his parents' failed marriage had done to Lynhurst Enterprises. He'd never repeat his father's mistakes. "The only reason to marry someone is if it gets you closer to where you want to be."

"I see. Marriage is your weapon. How romantic." She rolled her eyes. "Lucky me."

"Marriage is a tool," he corrected. "Romance is for losers who can't figure out how to get a woman into bed. I suffer from no such limitations."

"You might be surprised at what I consider romantic." She swept him with a heated once-over that slammed through him with knock-down, drag-out force.

"You're not going to be my wife in anything other than the legal sense. This is a strictly platonic deal, Meredith. I'm serious."

Her laugh rolled through him. "We'll see about that. It's not like you're suffering from a broken heart."

He had the distinct feeling he'd inadvertently challenged her to turn him into a liar. "So that means we're agreed?"

"I'll help you in exchange for the divorce, but only for a few weeks. I want twenty grand, not some measly minimum-wage salary. And you have to foot the bill for my hotel room."

He stuck out his hand and Meredith shook it. "Welcome to Lynhurst."

"Happy to be on board." She pulled him closer, skewering him with a sultry gaze. "What does a girl have to do to get the COO to take her to dinner?"

Three

Meredith spent Monday morning shopping at Barneys and cursed her meager credit limit. She'd packed a few days' worth of outfits for her unexpected trip to New York, not nearly enough for the two or three weeks she now planned to stay. And nothing in her suitcase would fly as a wardrobe for an employee at a high-class place like Hurst.

She still couldn't quite believe *she* had landed a job in a real fashion house. It was a dream come true, but one of those usually unattainable childhood dreams like becoming an astronaut or ballerina. And part of the dream was getting to dress the part.

Asking Jason for an advance on her salary would have invited too many questions, so she made do with the sale rack. Most of the clothes were out of season. She'd be outed as a fraud in a New York minute. No pun intended.

But still, it was a morning shopping at Barneys in Manhattan and life did not suck. Except for the part where she still didn't have the divorce papers signed…and she'd have to take an extended vacation from her job with her sister.

For the past two years, she'd assisted Cara as she designed and sold wedding dresses to Houston brides. Cara had recently begun selling her dresses in an upscale boutique and business was booming. Meredith wanted to make more of a contribution than simply as an assistant. What else could she do but buy in as a partner? Wedding dresses were Cara's first love and she excelled at the design side. Meredith might as well help on the financial side. She had little else to offer.

This was her chance to prove she had what it took. To prove everyone wrong who thought there wasn't anything more to Meredith than the stuff they saw on the outside.

Cara was in Barbados. Or was it Saint Martin? Meredith could never keep track of which resort her brother-in-law had dragged her sister to. Keith, her sister's husband, ran around the Caribbean fixing up resorts in his consultant job and Cara traveled with him. Hopefully she'd understand Meredith's need for time off without asking too many questions.

Meredith made a mental note to call her sister later.

Her phone buzzed and she keyed up the text message from Jason: Where are you? I'm at the hotel.

She texted him back: Shopping. Be back soon.

What was that all about? Was she supposed to sit around and wait for His Highness to appear? He might have his precious leverage—and she was still a little miffed about it, make no mistake—but that didn't mean Meredith planned to jump when he said jump.

When she got to the hotel after dallying an extra ten minutes just because, Jason was waiting for her in the lobby. He didn't notice her right away. Unashamedly, she watched him as he talked on the phone.

The man was unparalleled in the looks department. Clean-cut, gorgeous cheekbones, equally comfortable in a suit, jeans or nothing at all. It was enough to make a girl salivate.

And then he saw her. A smile spread across his face and sent a shiver down her spine.

Platonic was not going to happen. She was in New York for a couple of weeks, they were married, for God's sake, and they'd certainly had plenty of sex in the past. Why would he even say something so ridiculous?

They'd walked away from each other once and it hadn't worked out so well. It was time to try *not* walking away.

He pocketed his phone and stood.

"You should give me a key," he suggested when she met up with him as he strode toward the elevator.

"In case you want to make a middle-of-the-night visit to your wife? Because I'm totally okay with that."

He chuckled and stuck his palm against the open elevator door so Meredith could enter ahead of him. "Because I'm paying for the room. I might as well use it to make private phone calls instead of letting everyone in the lobby hear about Lyn's strategic plans."

Why was he so against resuming their relationship? It wasn't as if she was asking him to stay married—that wasn't what she wanted, either. Once she got herself established in a career, then she could think about whether she actually wanted to get married. Some women—like Cara—dreamed of nothing but white dresses and bouquets, but Meredith had never thought marriage was all that great of a goal.

Figuring out how to be a grown-up was the scary, frustrating can't-see-the-light-at-the-end-of-the-tunnel quandary Meredith couldn't dig her way out of. That goal felt as out of reach as it had two years ago.

She stuck her tongue out at him and fished the extra card key out of her purse, then handed it over. "Seems like a waste of a good hotel room to me. Sorry you had to hang out in the lobby, sugar, but perhaps you should have told me to expect you and I would have been here," she said without a trace of irony.

She hadn't heard from him all weekend. Not that she'd expected to.

He waved it off and followed her to her room. "I was in the neighborhood, so I came by to go over all the arrangements I've made for you at Hurst House."

"Already?" Her throat got a little tight as this Machia-vellian deal of Jason's got real.

What did she know about being a spy, in a fashion house or otherwise? The people at Jason's father's company would see through her instantly. If she failed at helping Jason get his plans back on track, would he refuse to sign the papers to spite her?

She should have gotten more of this established before she agreed. Actually, she should have told him no and demanded the divorce. But she well remembered how destroyed he'd been over the company splitting up, and she did have a *little* bit of fault in the marriage becoming legal in the first place, though how the paperwork had gotten submitted still baffled her. Her father's lawyer guessed that someone filed it on their behalf, probably a well-meaning hotel maid, but they'd never know for sure. Too much time had passed for anyone to remember.

She felt horrible about her part in it, and if she wished to prove she wasn't actually a scatterbrain, this was her opportunity. She couldn't abandon Jason. Adults took responsibility for mistakes and accepted consequences. Period.

"Yeah, already." His eyebrows went up. "You think I have time to waste? Avery doesn't rest, and she's too smart to underestimate. She'll have alternate plans in place in hopes of upstaging me. I can feel it."

"So what am I going to be doing?"

"You mentioned the other night at dinner that you'd been working as a designer's assistant. So it was a no-brainer to put you in that same role at Hurst House."

"Just like that?"

She would be working for a *God-honest designer*. If it was that easy to get a job working in the fashion industry in New York, could she have been doing it all along?

Her throat opened a little. At least she didn't have to learn a whole new job to be Jason's spy.

Except working with Cara was miles and miles away

from working with an established clothing label. Cara loved her and if Meredith occasionally messed up, it didn't feel like the end of the world. That's why buying into Cara's business was so important. It wasn't like Meredith could work with just anyone. It was the only opportunity available to her.

"Just like that. After I called my mother and asked her to recommend you, she called Hurst House Human Resources and informed them you'd be arriving tomorrow morning. The vice president of HR still has a guilt complex over defecting to Hurst House, so he'd pretty much do whatever my mom says."

"I see." How crazy was that? If only the rest of Meredith's appointed task went so easily. "And that's it? I show up, help one of the designers and wait around for Avery to stroll by? What if I never even see her?"

Why had she agreed to this again?

"You'll have to wing it. If you want the divorce badly enough, you'll figure out how to get the information I need."

Oh, so that's why he needed leverage. He didn't have any idea how this was supposed to go and hoped she'd be desperate enough to figure it out for him.

She snorted to cover her rising panic. "Lucky for you I'm a fast thinker."

"It's not luck." He shot her a strange look. "If I didn't think you could handle it, I never would have suggested this idea. You've got one of the sharpest minds of anyone I've ever met and I have no doubt you'll put your own spin on the assignment. In fact, I'm counting on it."

He thought she was smart. The revelation planted itself in her abdomen and spread with warm fingers. And of course, that alone motivated her in a way nothing else could. "You got it. I'm gonna be the best spy you've ever seen."

Jason was the only man who'd ever seen past her skin

to the real Meredith underneath. She'd never dreamed it would come to mean so much. Being here in his presence again, after all this time, had solidified why no other man did it for her.

But it had also brought home an ugly truth.

In Vegas, it had been okay to be clueless and spill all her uncertainty because Jason was at the same place. He'd grown up after coming home, like they'd planned. She hadn't. And that seemed to have everything to do with why he was so different.

She wanted the Jason of two years ago. And this unexpected extra time together gave her the perfect opportunity to peel back the layers of this new version of the man she'd married to see if she could find him again.

By ten o'clock the next morning, Meredith wished for a mocha latte, a bubble bath and that she'd never heard of Hurst House. Allo, the only-one-name-required in-house designer she'd been assigned to assist, hated her. Allo hated everyone as best Meredith could tell.

Allo called for shears yet again—the third time he'd changed his mind about whether he wanted chalk or shears—so Meredith trotted obediently to the table where all of Allo's tools had to be carefully stored when not in use. Even if he planned to use them in the next five minutes.

She placed the shears in Allo's outstretched hand and waited for the next round of barked instructions.

"Non, non, non." Allo threw the shears on the floor and kicked them across the beautiful blond hardwood. "I said pins. Take the cotton out of your head and pay attention."

"Pins. Coming right up," she muttered and cursed under her breath as she crossed to the cabinet yet again.

Tomorrow she'd wear flats. And bring cyanide to flavor Allo's chai tea. Not really, but she'd fantasized about it more than once after being told to remake the beverage four times.

Who was Meredith to question the genius of Allo, who had single-handedly launched Hurst House into the stratosphere with his line of ready-to-wear evening gowns? She'd even been a little tongue-tied when she'd first met him and secretly hoped she might absorb some of that genius. She still might. If she didn't kill him first.

None of Allo's assistants lasted longer than two months, according to the gossip she'd overheard in Human Resources that morning.

No wonder Bettina's phone call had netted Meredith a job so fast.

Now all she had to do was figure out how to casually run into Avery, pump her for secret information about her plans to thwart Jason's bid for CEO and then take over the world. Easy as pie.

At lunchtime, Meredith wearily contemplated the wilted salad and unidentifiable meat on offer in the building's cafeteria. The shopping trip to Barneys had been a wasted effort since everyone employed at Hurst House wore the Hurst House label, a small fact Jason could have mentioned. So her credit card was maxed out unnecessarily—though the off-the-shoulder Alexander Wang dress she'd found buried in the sale rack was amazing and she loved it. But having an amazing dress meant a low-cost and tasteless lunch.

All in the name of couture espionage.

"I wouldn't recommend the Salisbury steak."

Meredith glanced behind her and recognized Janelle, the girl from Human Resources who had performed Meredith's employee orientation. "Is that what it is? I wondered."

Janelle laughed. "They like to keep us guessing."

It was unusual to get such a friendly reception from another woman, and Meredith needed all the friends she could get if she hoped to score any information useful to Jason's cause. "What would you recommend for someone on a budget?"

Janelle pointed to the unrecognizable off-white lumps behind the Salisbury steak. "Chicken. Can't go wrong with that. It doesn't taste like anything in the first place, so it's hard to ruin it."

"Point taken." Meredith collected her lunch plate and inclined her head toward Janelle. "Any other first-day advice? I mean besides don't take a job working for Allo. That one I figured out on my own."

"Yeah, sorry about that." With a sympathetic smile, Janelle jerked her head in the direction of the dining room. "We made a pact in HR to do what we can to convince you to stay. Allo generates more paperwork for us than the tax department. Sit with me and I'll give you the scoop."

Oddly grateful for the support, Meredith followed Janelle to an unoccupied table as the other woman chatted about how to get around Allo's strident personality, how to win points and anything else she deemed worthwhile.

It wasn't until lunch was nearly over that Meredith got the break she'd been waiting for.

Janelle folded her napkin and glanced at her watch. "I've got to get back. I'll see you at the Garment Center gala tonight, right?"

"I don't know. What is it?"

"Samantha was supposed to invite you. I told her to send you an email with the details." Janelle looked annoyed. "Hurst House is a supporter of Save the Garment Center and there's a fund-raiser tonight. Avery Lynhurst—oh, she's the vice president of Marketing, if you haven't met her yet—is running the event and she wants all employees there. It makes her look good."

What better place to get in front of Jason's sister than a social event? And as a brand-new Hurst House employee, all the more reason to make sure she met everyone in attendance.

And it was a fashion-industry event that she got to attend. The thought made her downright cheerful.

"I'll be there," Meredith pledged and watched Janelle as she left the lunchroom.

As soon as Janelle was out of sight, she called Jason, who answered on the first ring.

"You have news, I trust?" he asked shortly, and the undercurrent said she was interrupting him, so she better make it good.

"There's an event tonight," she murmured softly in case anyone was listening in. "A Garment Center thing. Avery's going to be there, so I am, too. It's an opportunity to chat with her without raising any alarms."

"Excellent." Jason's voice warmed. "I'd forgotten about the gala, but you're right, it's perfect."

"There's one problem. I don't have anything to wear."

"That's the exact opposite of a problem," he said drily. "It so happens I know a couple of people in the evening-wear business. I'll swing by your hotel at six."

"You don't know what size I wear."

"Sweetheart, I'm a Lynhurst and that's plain insulting. Trust me," he advised with a chuckle. "See you tonight."

And that promise alone got her through the afternoon with Allo, the master of terror.

By tonight, she'd be one step closer to getting Jason's signature on the divorce papers. Then she could go back to Houston and get started on the rest of her grown-up life.

That had always been the plan. It should *still* be the plan. But she feared she'd spend the rest of her life dreaming of the man she'd divorced and continue to date lackluster men who couldn't begin to compare.

How had getting a man's signature on a piece of paper complicated everything so much?

Four

Jason pounded on the door of Meredith's hotel room for the fourth time and juggled the zipped garment bags. Again. When had he become an errand boy for a woman who'd probably never owned a clock in her life?

Enough was enough. He'd said six. It was six-oh-seven and Meredith *had* given him a key. And all the clothes he'd brought were heavy. If he didn't let himself in, they'd be late to the gala, and it would be more difficult to enter separately, keeping up the ruse that they didn't know each other.

But what if she was in the shower or blow-drying her hair in a little satin robe? One or the other was the most likely reason she hadn't heard his many knocks.

That decided it.

It would serve her right to gain an audience if she was naked in the bathroom. A guy could hope.

Bobbling the garment bags until his fingers closed around the card key in his pocket, he cleared the threshold and dumped his cargo on the bed. His wife strolled from the bathroom at the same moment, clad in nothing but a skimpy towel, revealing miles and miles of legs and toned arms.

All that bare skin seared his retinas. The full force of her slammed into the backs of his knees, weakening them dangerously. It was one thing to barge into a hotel room on the possible assumption the female occupant might be undressed; it was another to get his wish.

His tongue went numb and every drop of blood in his body drained into the instant bulge in his pants.

How could he have walked away from *that* in Vegas? He couldn't tear his gaze from her and a half whimper, half growl crawled out of his throat before he could stop it.

She didn't even have the grace to look startled or embarrassed.

"Hey, you," she called and pulled some frothy concoction of lace from her suitcase without censor, like men appeared in her bedroom unannounced on a regular basis.

Maybe they did. He frowned. Why did that thought make the back of his throat feel as if it was on fire?

"Uh, hey." He cleared his throat as she slid a foot into the sexy panties.

Instantly, he whirled to face the window. Apparently she intended to get dressed as if he wasn't even here. And what had he expected when he'd cavalierly charged into her room?

"Surely you're not shy all of a sudden. You've seen everything I've got and then some."

He could hear the smile in her voice. "It's the 'and then some' that's the problem," he muttered.

This was ridiculous. The thought of his wife with another man made him want to claw the paint off the walls, yet she wasn't really his wife and they were not going to repeat the craziness of the first round of their relationship. They *had* no relationship. And that's how it was going to stay.

She laughed. "You're wearing a tux. Are you going, too?"

"Yeah. You don't think I expect you to do this all on your own, do you?"

Of course, the plan to accompany her had formed well before she'd reminded him what happened when they spent more than five seconds in a room together. Abrupt loss of focus. Instant desire to do nothing more than spend several hours in bed, with Meredith's soft laugh and softer skin against his.

The woman turned him stupid instantly.

"What, you don't trust me?" she asked coquettishly. "I'm dressed. You can stop pretending to have some misguided sense of modesty."

"I'm not pretending. Just because we're married doesn't mean I should get a free show."

He turned to face the interior of the room and got an eyeful of Meredith's idea of *dressed*—a bra-and-panty set skimpy enough that it should be illegal. God, she was going to kill him.

The freaking bath towel had covered more flesh. Her smile said she knew exactly what she was doing to him.

"Honey, you can fantasize about keeping this platonic to your heart's content. Just don't hold it against me if I give you something else to fantasize about." She raised her eyebrows suggestively. "What did you bring me?"

A hard-on the size of a subway train, apparently. "Clothes. I don't remember what."

She huffed out a sigh. "I'll check it out myself, then."

This heightened sense of awareness was merely the product of the close confines and distinct lack of sex over the past few months. Maybe if he could get a dress on her, and they got the hell out of this very private hotel room, he could breathe again.

Obviously, he had more in common with his hormonally driven father than Jason would have liked.

She unzipped the garment bag on top of the pile and squealed. "Oh, Jason."

His name in her throaty come-and-get-me voice washed over him, tightening the already massive erection he probably wasn't hiding as well as he hoped.

Who was he kidding? It didn't matter if they left the

hotel room; this evening was going to suck regardless because he couldn't think about anything *but* sex where Meredith was concerned.

He put some steel in his spine and pulled the glittery dress from the hanger. "It's one of Allo's. *Vogue* revealed it in a spread last week, but it's not in stores yet. I thought you might like to be the first woman to wear it out."

"What?" Her mouth gaped. "*Me?* You want me to wear a just-revealed dress designed by Allo to a *fashion-industry* event?"

Undisguised glee radiated from her expression and he forgot what he'd been about to say. Why did pleasing her make him feel as if *he'd* been given a gift?

"Put it on," he said, his voice husky and foreign. He cleared his throat. "I want to see it on you."

She complied, sliding her lithe legs through the opening at the top and gathering it into place against her torso. Then she presented her back, lifted her dark fall of gorgeous hair away and called over her shoulder, "Zip me up?"

Since his fingers were already straining for the zipper before she'd finished speaking, it seemed the answer was yes. He crossed to her and her heat reached out to engulf him. Slowly, he skated the zipper up its track, following the line of her bare flesh above it with his gaze.

Wrong way, his brain screamed. *Unzip! Unzip!*

He resisted. Barely. But his fingers wouldn't let go of the zipper pull, even though the dress was as zipped as it could be. Meredith's exotic perfume wrapped around him and somehow, his nose was nearly buried in her still-damp hair. It smelled like green apple. He sucked in a breath and the combination of scents and the essence of *her* wove through his senses.

She swayed, brushing his arousal with her shapely rear. He sought the curve of her waist, meaning to push her forward a step but instead rested his hands there as he drew her backward, flush with his body. Her head tipped back against his shoulder and she moaned so sexily, the answering spike of lust nearly blinded him.

So he shut his eyes and let his lips trail down her exposed throat. She tasted decadent and sinful and he wanted to sink into her.

"Jason," she murmured and twisted in his arms to peer up at him, her gaze heavy with unconcealed desire.

The kiss they'd shared roared back on a wave of unsuppressed memory and he ached to lay his lips on hers again. Her face tipped up, bringing her mouth within centimeters of his and paradise was within his reach.

But then she murmured his name again and said, "I'm absolutely okay with being really late to the gala. But are you?"

Rationality swamped him and cooled his ardor in a snap. "Yeah, no. Not really."

He stepped back. Meredith's mystifying and infuriating pull on him hadn't diminished, that was for sure. He didn't like it when someone had that much leverage over him, especially when he couldn't envision how she'd use it to her advantage.

Best-case scenario, she'd use it to get him into bed and leave it at that. He didn't ever count on best-case scenarios and besides, she'd have to try a lot harder to break his will.

His subconscious dissolved into gales of laughter and then reminded him that *she'd* been the one to halt what had almost turned into an invigorating reintroduction to the pleasures of his wife's body.

"All right, then." She smiled softly and he ignored the slight hitch it put in his gut. "Stop being so sexy and we'll have a much better shot of getting through the door."

He rolled his eyes. "The rest of the clothes are for you, too. I heard a rumor that you made a faux pas by wearing Alexander Wang your first day on the job. Allo is jealous of him. He wanted that Balenciaga job that Wang landed."

If Jason had known that weasel of a vice president in HR

would stick Meredith with Allo, he'd have specified otherwise. Too late now. He couldn't risk pulling any strings to get her reassigned or someone might get suspicious. But he could help her earn some points with her extremely difficult boss and the new clothes would accomplish that like nothing else. Allo was a narcissist to the core.

Meredith raised a brow. "Why, exactly, did you need me as a spy when you apparently already have plenty?"

"Nobody gossips about anything relevant to my merger plans." He waved a dismissive hand. "Only what people are wearing. Welcome to the world of fashion. And now you have a wardrobe worthy of the design floor at Hurst House."

The new wardrobe was also a bit of a thank-you, and he hoped she liked what he'd painstakingly picked out among the castoffs from Fashion Week.

"Wait, there's more than this dress? I figured the other bags held backups in case this one didn't fit." Meredith dug through the garment bags and squealed some more over the geometric dresses, skirts and angular tops from Hurst's newest line. None of it was available in stores yet, either.

"There you go insulting me again. You can try all of it on later," Jason advised. "We should leave. I have an out-of-the-way place in mind for a quick dinner. I'm sorry I can't take you to Nobu, or some place you might enjoy more, but we can't chance being photographed together."

She gave him an indecipherable look. "You don't have to take me to dinner at all. We're not dating. Just married."

"Which is why I should take you to dinner. Don't you think a wife should be treated better than a woman I'm simply dating?"

"Well…yeah." She tossed the four-hundred-dollar V-neck silk blouse on the bed. "But I thought you were Mr. No-Romance. Marriage is a tool, you said. I'm here to help you get a boring executive's job so you'll sign the divorce papers."

Romance? Dinner wasn't a precursor to seduction. Why was he torturing himself like this again? He threw up his hands. "Fine. Don't eat, then. We'll go to the gala and I'll shove you out of the car three blocks away so you can walk. Sound like a plan?"

"Good thing for you new clothes put me in a forgiving mood. So I'll overlook your bad attitude." As she stepped into a pair of sky-high stilettos—Miu Miu unless he missed his guess—she shot him a sunny smile. "And I would love to go to dinner. Thank you for asking."

Point taken. He groaned. "Meredith, would you like to go to dinner?"

She crossed to him and patted his cheek. "Maybe you should take some husband lessons if you hope to marry someone for real. Because, honey, you're obviously out of practice. For someone who thinks of marriage as a tool, you sure haven't figured out how to use it yet."

Her husky voice put plenty of innuendo in the statement, making it crystal clear she thought he was a moron for not taking advantage of what she was offering.

He followed her out of the hotel room and prayed her next suggestion wasn't an offer to be his tutor. Because he had the horrible feeling he might accept.

The third glass of champagne disappeared much more quickly than the second, and Meredith forced herself not to reach for a fourth. Avery Lynhurst still hadn't made an appearance and if Meredith was forced to watch another supermodel hit on Jason, she couldn't be held responsible for her actions.

It was bad enough that she couldn't keep her eyes off him. And worse, he didn't seem to be similarly afflicted. It was as if she didn't exist.

Meredith smiled at the buyer for Nordstrom who'd been chatting her up for ten minutes. Some of the most powerful people in the New York fashion scene milled about in the Grand Ballroom of the iconic Plaza hotel and it was a bit dizzying to be in the midst of it.

Everyone in attendance dazzled in top-tier labels, and she voraciously soaked in the visual panorama. One lucky woman had somehow scored a Galinda Gennings gown adorned with real diamonds.

A hush fell on Meredith's right, but she didn't think anything of it until the crowd parted and Allo appeared on a tide of arrogance and condescending flair. She stifled a groan. Wasn't it bad enough that she had to spend eight hours a day being chastised? She deserved a night off.

"You." The designer waved his hand in Meredith's direction. "You're fired. See HR in the morning to get your exit papers."

What had she done now? A cold skitter went down her spine. Had someone seen her get out of Jason's car? They'd been so careful, separating on 58th Street a full two blocks from the hotel.

Allo's entourage tittered meanly and waited for the next round of fireworks with expectant expressions.

"Why?" Meredith narrowed one eye. "I did a great job working for you today. If you didn't think so, why didn't you say something earlier?"

"Non." Allo pursed his lips and muttered something in French that sounded uncomplimentary. "You have stolen my dress. You are a thief. That is the reason for your termination."

Meredith glanced down at the glittery dress Jason had given her. "This? You think I stole it?"

Crap. Why hadn't she and Jason discussed a good cover story? Of course a designer's brand-new assistant wouldn't have access to a dress that wasn't in stores yet. The photographers outside the ballroom had gone wild when Meredith hit the red carpet and she'd reveled in it a bit more than she probably should have. It had lulled her into a false sense of belonging that she clearly hadn't earned yet.

Meredith shook her head, thoughts racing. If she got fired, she couldn't be Jason's spy and there went her divorce. He'd never sign the papers if she screwed up this fast.

"I would never insult you like that, Allo," she countered smoothly. *Thank you, Miss Texas pageant, for training me how to brazen it out under the worst sort of pressure.* "I begged, uh…Samantha for this dress. It was on the rack in the…"

Which room at Hurst held the outfits for photo shoots? Someone had shown it to her during her orientation, but she'd been too busy gushing over the clothes to notice her surroundings. Meredith snagged a glass of champagne from a passing waiter and offered it to Allo as the name came to her.

"West gallery," she lied brightly. With no clue where Jason had actually scored the dress, she had to wing it. "I immediately recognized it as yours, and you're such a genius, I knew I couldn't wear anything else tonight. Only Allo will do for me from now on. The press ate it up."

"Of course they did." Allo sniffed, accepting the glass as if he'd asked for it thirty minutes ago and Meredith had been slow to fetch it. "You're too short to do that bit of brilliance justice, by the way. Don't be late tomorrow. We have much work to do."

He sailed off into the crowd and Meredith shook her head. Crisis averted. For now. "See you around, boss."

From behind her, Jason's warm chuckle flowed over her like honey.

"Don't turn around," he murmured.

"Why, because you don't want anyone to know I'm talking to you?" Meredith guessed and clamped down on the hard twist of need his presence had generated. He wasn't close enough to feel, but she could sense him, as if his heat had wrapped around her.

"Because I find myself entranced by your back."

"Yeah, you seem to have a thing for zippers." She bit

her lip as awareness ratcheted up a notch with the memory of his body behind hers as he'd helped her dress earlier.

He'd been hard and delicious, and while he might be lying to himself about not being into her, his erection against her backside had told her the plain, honest truth. He wanted her. And she wanted him. Sex between them had been mind-altering. Explosive. Unmatched.

So why all the theatrics over whether they'd eventually end up in bed? It was pretty much a foregone conclusion in her mind. Once she got him between the sheets, they'd laugh over private jokes and share their souls and he'd remember how great it had been in Vegas.

Maybe they wouldn't have to end things so quickly this time.

Jason cleared his throat. "Good thinking with Allo. It was impressive."

"Yeah, well you owe me." A spiky little thrill in her midsection that had nothing to do with sex surprised her. She'd been trying to save her job, but Jason's approval meant more than it should.

"Avery just waltzed in. Showtime."

Jason's heat vanished. By all rights, they should have been vanishing through the door together to make out in the car on the way back to her hotel room, where the big, lonely bed would actually be used for its rightful purpose.

All at once, it wasn't sex she craved, but the totally foreign desire to fall asleep in Jason's arms, like she had in Vegas, knowing they'd wake up together in the morning in perfect sync. Back then, they'd shared some kind of mystical connection that she desperately missed.

"See you around, boss," she muttered for the second time with a mental salute.

Here in New York, he wasn't on her side. In this sea of people, she was alone. It wasn't the two of them against the world, supporting each other and dreaming of how the future could look. All of that seemed to have been left behind in the desert.

Maybe he'd changed more than she'd been willing to admit. Was that why she couldn't find her footing with him?

Maybe he was right about keeping things platonic. The last thing she wanted was to get naked with Jason again, only to have her perfect fantasy destroyed by reality.

Sadness cut through her heart. She was chasing a man who didn't exist any longer. She had to stop wishing for something that wasn't going to happen. Get the intel, get the divorce and get home so she could ask her father for a loan—that was her purpose here. This was nothing more than a job.

It was bad enough to have one person to answer to. In actuality, she had two. And she didn't like either one of them at the moment. She elbowed her way through the crowd until she caught sight of Jason's sister.

Meredith pasted on her best I'm-the-answer-to-all-your-prayers smile and approached Avery Lynhurst. The blonde woman oozed style and class in her Hurst House gown and emanated the warmth of a barracuda. She and Jason shared similar features, mostly around the mouth and eyes, and they both had that sharp, attentive air as if neither of them missed an iota of what happened around them. Meredith had a feeling Avery used the information she gathered to get what she wanted just as effectively as Jason did.

Avery was indeed a formidable opponent to Jason's plans.

"Ms. Lynhurst, I'm Meredith Chandler-Harris." Meredith shook the other woman's hand as Avery took her measure. "I'm Allo's new assistant."

"Yes, I know." With a toss of her white-blond hair, Avery swept Meredith with a condescending glance. "Nice of you to deign to wear the label of the house that signs your paychecks."

Meredith smiled as she clamped her back teeth together to keep the snarl from escaping. "Wearing Wang to the office today was a rookie mistake. I'm a fast learner, obviously."

Avery nodded to Meredith's dress. "That's one of my favorites. It's not my color, though."

To anyone else, Avery's comment would have seemed downright friendly, but Meredith had spent years in the trenches with pageant contestants and she recognized the need to tread carefully. Avery wasn't complimenting her, that was for sure.

"But only you could pull off that particular Allo." As she eyed Avery's dress, Meredith fixed the most appreciative and slightly jealous look on her face possible. "He designed it with you in mind, clearly. And his inspiration was well-founded."

"Yes, well." Avery cocked her head. "Where did you work before coming to Hurst House? I know every designer and designer's assistant in Manhattan. You're not from here."

"I'm from Houston." And the name Chandler-Harris meant nothing in New York, so Meredith didn't bother to toss in a mention of her connections. "I worked for a bridal design company. I feel truly blessed to have a chance to work for a top-notch label like Hurst House."

"Hurst is a long way from wedding dresses."

The disdain was thick. Meredith enjoyed working for Cara and liked wedding dresses, but she flicked a hand and bit back the name she'd really like to call Avery. "Honey, that scene is so limited. You know. Same fabrics, same colors. Same indecisive brides. This is where all the action is. Designers at Hurst House know what they want and how to do it and don't let anyone stand in their way. I'd like to learn that."

Avery's eyes glittered brighter than Meredith's dress. "Interesting. You're the first designer's assistant I've met who understands fashion is about more than the clothes. It's about owning your designs. No apologies."

Nodding, Meredith went with it, though it was really the first time she'd articulated how she felt about the fashion industry. "That's what makes working for Allo so amazing. You can feel the energy in the room. When he's creating, he makes no mistakes. It's brilliant simply because he believes that it is."

Avery seemed intrigued for God knew what reason.

"You know, if you're eager to learn from a mentor, I'm working on a project and I need a fresh perspective." Avery evaluated Meredith coolly. "It's hush-hush, though. I need someone who doesn't mind long, grueling hours far past the time regular people go home. I call the shots, you listen and follow my instructions to the letter. It's a chance to see what really goes on at a major house like Hurst. Behind the scenes. Interested?"

Not for any amount of money did she want to hole up in Avery's office at midnight. Especially since she had a sneaking suspicion Avery had only made the offer to keep an eye on her. Meredith must have tripped Avery's radar somehow. Why else would Jason's sister waste an opportunity like this on a new hire?

But Jason was paying her in currency far more valuable than mere money, and this was her golden opportunity to keep an eye on Avery in turn, regardless of the woman's suspicious motives. "I'm your girl. Long hours don't scare me. I don't even own a watch."

"I'll be in touch. You'll keep working for Allo, but we'll come to some agreement about your after-hours compensation. Welcome to Hurst House." Avery smiled and excused herself.

And now Meredith had three bosses. Four if you counted Cara, who was patiently waiting for Meredith to rejoin the wedding-dress business.

Meredith's head swam. For a woman who'd been floundering, she certainly seemed to have found a life raft full of opportunities.

Five

Meredith and Avery talked far longer than Jason would have ever put money on. And Avery looked far too satisfied with the conversation for his comfort.

What were they saying to each other? Had Avery dropped any worthwhile information into the mix? No. Surely not. She'd just met Meredith, and Avery wasn't much of a blabbermouth. Everything she did came about through careful calculation.

Finally, his sister and Meredith parted, and Avery's smile was enigmatic and dangerous. He didn't like it. Anytime his sister smiled, it made him nervous.

His mother snapped her fingers in his face. "Earth to Jason."

"Sorry. I'm a little distracted." He refocused on Bettina and tried to put Meredith out of his mind.

With an indulgent smile, Bettina swirled her club soda and lime. "Yes, that's certainly one way to describe Avery's gorgeous new friend. As I was saying…"

She launched into a lengthy speech about ideas for her new swimwear line targeted at younger girls. Jason offered a half-formed opinion, wondering how his mother had known he was watching Meredith when he'd been careful to give everyone the opposite impression. Obviously, he was slipping.

Swimwear. That's what he needed to be thinking about.

Bettina had been running the company for two years and was ready to jump back into the design side. Perfect timing, in Jason's mind. If she eased away from her CEO role, he could slide right into the gap, ready to take over and execute his merger plans. His mother needed confidence in him and a new project to keep her busy.

Then Meredith left the ballroom in a swish of glittery dress and mahogany hair and Jason left his mother midsentence with a terse, "Be right back."

He had to know what Avery said to Meredith. The suspense was killing him.

Meredith ducked into the ladies' room, forcing Jason to cool his heels in the hall. He sipped his martini and tried to pretend he was getting some air.

When Meredith's distinctive dress flashed in his peripheral vision, he tilted his head toward the opposite end of the hall, away from the ballroom. He strolled in that direction without looking over his shoulder to be sure she was following him. She better be.

He turned the corner and lucked into a small alcove with a plush bench and side table. It was empty. Meredith's exotic perfume hit him a moment before the most striking woman in attendance appeared. The one-two punch put him on edge.

"What's up?" she asked. "Isn't meeting like this a little risky?"

He conceded the point with a small nod. "Yeah. So talk fast. What did Avery say?"

"Maybe you should learn the art of patience, hmm?" She perched on the edge of the bench and made a big show of fixing a buckle on her shoe.

"Don't be difficult. You talked to her for a long time. Avery doesn't chat. She strategizes. What angle did she play?"

Meredith flipped her hair behind her back and stole Jason's martini, which she downed in one gulp. "Pot, meet kettle."

"What's that supposed to mean?"

She arched a brow. "It means you two are cut from the same cloth, no pun intended. Maybe you should stop thinking about the angles once in a while."

With a growl, he snatched the empty glass from his wife's hand and checked his temper before he slammed it down on the side table and shattered it into a million pieces. Which might ease his frustration but wouldn't get the answers out of Meredith any faster. "What is your problem? I'm asking you to give me information. That's why you're here, Meredith."

"No, that's why *you're* here, darling." She raked him with a smoldering once-over that lit him up instantly. "I have my own reasons for agreeing to this stupid plan of yours."

His scowl didn't faze her and her calm rattled his cage even further. "Is this another cheap ploy to get me to hop into bed with you? Because it's getting a little old. Why can't you get it through your head that I'm not interested?"

Quickly, she smoothed the hurt from her expression. If he hadn't been so focused on her face, he would have missed it. Instantly, his ire drained away. "I'm sorry. That was uncalled for. Avery drives me mental."

It was a poor excuse and not fully accurate. Oh, his sister had her moments, but he'd never had any problem keeping his cool around *her*. It was his wife who altered his brain waves with merely a glance.

"It's fine." She waved it away dismissively, but her tone said it was anything but fine. "I decided you're right. Sleeping together would be a mistake. Much cleaner to stay out of bed and get through this as quickly as possible. No reason to complicate something that's already complicated enough."

Well, well. He was finally getting through to her. "Glad you see the wisdom."

He waited for a sense of relief. And kept waiting.

What had prompted this turnabout anyway? He didn't understand her motivation for her invitation to pick up where they'd left off in the first place, and he *really* didn't understand her motivation for backing off now. He had to know why.

Right after she spilled about Avery.

"Is there more you can get out of Avery tonight? If no, maybe we should go," Jason suggested.

Once they got back to her hotel, the stress of being caught together would be off and then he could pick through her strange mood until she told him what he wanted to know.

"No, my work here is done," she said flatly and stood. "I'll catch a cab back to my hotel. No need to see me out since this isn't a date. Later, Tater."

With the sarcasm of her parting comment still echoing through the alcove, she sailed down the hall without a backward glance. Jason barely got his mouth closed fast enough to scramble after her.

But not too closely. He slowed a bit as he passed the ballroom full of his colleagues and nodded to his father without stopping. *Nobody* would think it was strange they didn't exchange a word. Jason hadn't spoken to Paul in about six months and they both preferred it that way.

By the time he reached the sidewalk outside the hotel, Meredith had disappeared into a cab. He swore and signaled to his driver to get the car.

Where did she think she was going? She couldn't hide from him—he had a key to her room.

"Now this seems familiar," he muttered as he pounded on Meredith's hotel-room door for the second time that evening.

"What?" she called from inside the room.

"Candygram."

"Go away. I'm about Lynhursted out for the day."

"Come on, let me in so we can have a rational discussion like adults. If that's even possible."

The door flew open. "What kind of a crack is that? You think I can't act like an adult?"

At least she was still dressed. A small blessing, though that glittery dress with the tiny spaghetti straps and deep V over her cleavage had made him fantasize about unzipping it all night.

He pushed into the room, ignoring her protests, and went straight for the minibar. A fifteen-dollar shot of Jack Daniel's sounded like a bargain. The liquor slid down his throat and soothed his temper enough to allow a response. "That comment was directed at both of us. We're apparently only capable of insulting each other and I'd like to find a way to get past it."

She planted herself an inch from him, fists at her hips. "And *I'd* like a divorce. Maybe we can trade."

He threw up his hands. "Yet you stormed off from the gala when all I was trying to do was get us to the divorce faster."

Something shiny glinted in her expression and he did a double take. He'd never seen Meredith cry. She was a woman of many extremes, but sadness wasn't one of them. It threw him for a loop. His first response was to pull her into his arms and murmur nonsense into her hair.

She stiffened for a second and then liquefied against him, her arms snaking into place at his waist. Her head tilted against his shoulder, resting in a groove that had been waiting for her to fill it. Sniffling, she let him cradle her and the tension eased.

He pulled back so he could look into her eyes, the only way he knew to assess a person. The tears were still there, but she had a little of her normal snap back, too. His heart slowed.

"I don't pretend to be good at relationships, and we're

not even in one. But obviously I'm messing up whatever it is that we're doing here. Can't you give me some clues what I'm doing wrong?"

She sighed and slipped from his embrace, which grew cool far too fast. Surprising how quickly he'd gotten used to her heat.

"That's just it, Jason. I don't think you're doing anything wrong. This is who you are and I'm not above admitting I'm bitterly disappointed."

"Wait a minute." The buzzing in his ears didn't clear even with a hard shake of his head. "You're disappointed in who I *am*?"

Meredith evaluated him for a long, tense moment. "The man I met in Vegas wasn't so cold and calculating. He was passionate and open and I loved being around him."

She crossed to the bar and found her own fifteen-dollar shot of Jack Daniel's.

"He was also confused and misguided," Jason added. And that guy had been heavily under the influence of Meredith's seductive power. "I'd like to think you helped get me to the place where I am now. I owe you a debt for that, as a matter of fact."

She rolled her eyes and splashed Sprite in her highball along with the amber liquid, then downed it in two gulps.

"Great, so I get the credit for turning you into a zombie." She plunked the glass down and pierced him with her still-shiny gaze. "You want to know what Avery said to me? She asked me to work on a special project with her. After hours."

Elation warmed the cold place Meredith had left behind. "That's fantastic. It's perfect. You play your cards right and she might start to trust you. You can cozy up to her and get far more information about her plans."

"It's not perfect!" She poked a finger in his chest. "It's not even for real as best I can tell. You know why she asked me to work with her? She's keeping me close because she can't figure out my angle. I'm from Houston and have a background in bridal design. What am I doing horning in on New York couture, she asked."

Inwardly, he winced. They should have thought of a good cover story. Too late now.

"It's a logical question." How had Meredith figured out Avery's motivation so quickly?

He cursed as it dawned on him that Avery might be aware of his relationship with Meredith. Was that the reason behind the offer? "What did you tell her?"

Meredith was smart and quick on her feet. Their plans could still work.

"I told her exactly what she wanted to hear. Because I did not want to mess up a golden opportunity. The goal is for me to help you, right?"

"Of course. So thanks." Why did it sound like the incident had upset her?

She muttered a very unladylike curse. "Geez, Jason. You don't get it. I'm standing there listening to her talk and all I could think about was how the two of you are exactly alike. Cold-blooded and only interested in one-upping each other. And both of you are thrilled to use me to do it."

"I'm not using you," Jason protested instantly. He and Avery were not alike. He always used a situation to his advantage, but he wasn't taking advantage of *Meredith*. "We have a deal. You get something out of it, too, and I wouldn't even have the divorce to use as leverage if you hadn't allowed the papers to get filed."

Suddenly, he felt like a heel. He didn't like the thought of Meredith being disappointed in him, either. He hadn't always been so cold, but it was a necessity in the cutthroat world of fashion.

Nice guys finished last. And they didn't manage hostile mergers or win CEO spots away from their conniving sisters.

She strangled over a disgusted sound and leaned in, indignation sweeping through her expression. "There you go again. This marriage is not all my fault. You stood in front of that Elvis impersonator with me. *You.* I didn't drag you to the altar. If I recall, it was your idea."

He stepped back, away from her prodding finger, away from her anger and, most important, away from the truth. "Yeah, I can man up and admit it. I made a mistake in the heat of the moment."

She advanced on him again, charging into the space he'd created and bringing her sensual onslaught with her. "I'll say. And that moment was smoking hot. You can pretend that this—" she waved stiff fingers in a circle around Jason's tuxedoed torso "—is the place you were trying to get to, but I know the real you. The one you hide under this rigid CEO exterior. The man under there doesn't have a problem acknowledging his passion. He owns it, takes what he wants. That's the man I spent two years dreaming about."

Mesmerized, he watched the flicker in Meredith's gaze flare into something far hotter than any sane man should touch.

"Yeah? What do you dream about?"

That had not been what he'd meant to say. He cleared his throat, but it was too late. It was already out there.

"Your mouth." She reached up and traced it with her index finger, and his flesh sparked under her touch. "Your abs. The way you sigh after you come. The way my fingers look in your hair when you're under me."

Her fingers wound through his hair in a full-on demonstration. His body strained to close the small gap between them, begging to feel her one last time.

She was trying to goad him into losing his careful guard. It wasn't going to work. "I thought you didn't want to complicate this with sex."

"It's already so complicated it couldn't get much worse." Her smile turned wicked. "And I said that before you chased me back to my hotel room. Are you sure *you* know what you want?"

The smartest thing to do would be to keep his mouth shut. Because she'd called it—his middle name should be Mixed Signals. "Yeah. I know exactly what I want."

"Me, too. I want that man," she murmured. "Inside and out. I want to know it wasn't all a lie, that I don't misremember how amazing we were together. I want you inside me and to be so far from disappointed, I forget the meaning of the word."

The undisguised longing in her voice, in her touch, found the answering longing inside him. He hadn't realized it was there, waiting for her to unearth it, but it flared to life nonetheless. And in that moment, he wanted to give her what she wanted, to erase her disillusionment and embrace the devil-may-care Jason of Vegas again.

Would it really be so bad to indulge in a few hours of Meredith, burn it out of their systems and go back to real life tomorrow?

Yes, it would. Because he wasn't that man she remembered. That wasn't the real Jason Lynhurst. He'd only dabbled on the wild side because he'd been so messed up. Only that unique combination of confusion and Meredith could have enticed him to act so unlike himself and so much like his father.

Meredith's odd sway over him would only intensify if he gave in now. There would be no going back to real life once he tasted her particular brand of recklessness again. And then she'd use every bit of his weakness to her advantage. That he could never allow—he had a vision for the future of Lynhurst Enterprises and it did not involve Meredith. It would be unfair to her to let her believe he could be the man she seemed to want.

"It was a lie," he said. "You misremember. We can never get Vegas back and it would be madness to try."

He nearly choked on the words and immediately wished

he'd said something else, anything else. Because he knew good and well it wasn't a lie and she didn't misremember.

Worst of all, he wanted it, too. Wanted to indulge in a woman who made him feel, made him forget. An oasis of connection and understanding far removed from the ugly battles playing out across the remnants of Lynhurst Enterprises.

She banked the hurt in her gaze and nodded. "See ya. Don't call me. I'll call you."

Meredith gave up on the idea of sleeping at around 2:00 a.m. Tomorrow—correction, *today*—already promised to be brutal since she'd spend hours in Allo's torture chamber. But coupled with no sleep and Jason's thorough rejection, she might as well get on a plane back to Houston.

Surely a conversation with her father in which she admitted her mistake in Vegas and begged his forgiveness would be easier than the ups and downs of Jason's deal. The worst part was she'd known what would happen last night when she went for broke. But she'd done it anyway because she couldn't stop herself.

She yearned for the thrill Jason evoked when he slid into her and the kinship they'd shared. Then there was the communication and affinity—they'd had it all once upon a time, and for some reason, he refused to acknowledge how great the two of them naked had been.

But what if the Jason she couldn't forget never surfaced? Hanging on to that fantasy was the surest path to never moving on.

She slogged through the day, earning cutting remarks from Allo without even trying, a real bonus that went well with her mood. Avery never contacted her, and in an apparent attempt to give her what she'd asked for, Jason didn't call, either.

When she got back to her hotel, she booted up her laptop in an attempt to distract herself from the day, and an email from her mother put the cap on a supremely awful day. Thought you might want to see this, the note said and included a link to an online article titled: Miss Texas— Where Is She Now?

Dread knotted Meredith's stomach as she clicked the link. Exactly as she expected, a professional head shot from her pageant days filled the screen alongside the photos of two other women. She recognized Brandi MacArthur and LaTisha Kelley easily. Brandi had handed over her crown to Meredith when she won. And the following year, Meredith had handed her crown to LaTisha.

Kicking off her heels, Meredith sank down in the plush chair, determined to read every word on the screen.

The article wasn't a smear job or a puff piece. It was a well-written factual chronicle of the three women's lives since their respective reigns ended. Brandi was now a neonatal neurosurgeon working at the Baylor University Medical Center in Dallas, married to David Thomason, the renowned heart-transplant specialist. LaTisha had taken a different path, receiving a master's degree in theology and then signing on to become a missionary in Haiti. The writer expanded on their achievements in several glowing paragraphs, highlighting that the Miss Texas pageant had opened doors for these ladies, which they had walked through to enormous success.

Meredith's sole mention painted a sad but true picture— "Meredith Chandler-Harris works for her sister and is a second-generation Miss Texas. Her mother, Valerie Chandler, won the title in the eighties."

The article was kind enough to leave out the part where Meredith hadn't achieved a tenth of what her fellow titleholders had. But it was implied quite well.

Her mother hadn't sent the link to be malicious. She probably saw nothing wrong with the fact that of the two lines devoted to her daughter, fifty percent were about Valerie. As a major contributor to the Houston social scene, her mother thought nothing of seeing her name in print.

She also didn't have a shred of ambition. But Meredith, unlike her mother, had always wanted to be more than a wife to someone important. The Grown-Up Pact was supposed to help Meredith figure out what she might be good at besides smiling and traipsing down a runway.

Instead, she'd left Vegas hung up on a man who didn't long to recreate their connection the way she did. He'd rather lie about whether it had existed in the first place.

Perhaps part of her problem with not embracing her inner adult lay in being so stuck in the past. She sighed. She should really let Fantasy Jason go, get Real-Life Jason's signature on the divorce papers and move on.

Her cell phone beeped, and when she tapped open the new text message, her brow arched. It was from Jason, with the simple question: Thai for dinner?

Like last night hadn't even happened?

Of course. Because in his mind, it was business as usual.

Two could play that game. In fact, she'd do herself a favor if she played the game his way and left her emotions out of it.

She texted him back: With plenty of red pepper sauce.

Jason replied: Be there in fifteen minutes.

She couldn't stop a tiny tendril of hope that dinner might be some kind of apology. A way to say, "Hey, I was just kidding. You rocked me in Vegas and I couldn't forget it even with brain damage."

He made it in ten, and when he swept into her hotel room looking devastating in his grey custom-made Lyn Couture suit, with spiky hair in delicious disarray, her heart fell out of rhythm and she couldn't breathe for a moment.

So much for leaving her emotions at the door.

"How was your day, dear?" she asked a touch more sarcastically than she probably should have, but her not-quite-a-husband had thrown her off balance.

He shot her a grimace. "We have a problem. Come eat and I'll tell you about it."

Oh. Of course that was the reason for his appearance so soon after the disaster of last night. She tossed the laptop onto the bed.

Meredith took the take-out box from Jason's hand and opened it. Pad Thai shrimp. It was her favorite, but far be it from her to read into the selection. There was no way Jason remembered that. Lots of people loved pad Thai. Jason had used his finely honed observation skills to make a good guess, that was all.

Listlessly, she picked at the food, washing down what little she could stomach with a beer Jason had retrieved from the minibar.

"What's the problem?" she asked.

"Avery put the first part of what must be her plan in motion today." Jason forked up a mouthful of his red curry beef and took his sweet time chewing. "Several reporters were tipped off to investigate potential labor violations against Lyn's factory workers. The press ambushed Bettina as she was leaving the office today, shouting for comments about how she was running a sweatshop right here in Manhattan."

Meredith scowled. "That's ridiculous. I hope Bettina put them in their place."

It wasn't like she *really* knew it wasn't true, but Jason was the chief operating officer and there was no way he'd abuse his factory workers. Nor would he let someone else force workers to endure difficult conditions.

Jason flashed a brief, grateful smile and sobered almost immediately. "I wish she had. But she's not a spokesperson. Put her in a room with reams of fabric and she's good for hours. Talking to the press, not so much. The whole thing upset her."

"And you think Avery was behind this?"

"I'd put money on it."

He dropped his fork and took a long pull from his beer, massaging the back of his neck as he swallowed. Tension put fine lines around his mouth and eyes, sullying his classically handsome face, and she could do without that.

Dropping her own fork, she stood and scooted around behind him to replace his hand with hers, kneading his taut neck muscles for him. He groaned appreciatively and his head tipped back.

"You don't have to do that," he murmured. "Don't you dare stop."

She laughed. "I wasn't going to. Your muscles are like concrete. Relax for a minute."

She wouldn't have realized how tense he was if she hadn't felt it with her own two hands. He'd been hiding it well, at least until these past couple of minutes.

Which of course led her down the path of wondering what else he was hiding under that gorgeous suit. He was a man of contrasts. Frustrating to be sure, but oh, so intriguing. She wanted to dig into his core in the worst way and expose all his secrets…like, why was he so resistant to being open and passionate as he'd been in Vegas? It wasn't her—his body's reaction anytime they got within two feet of each other gave her all the assurance she needed.

If only he'd bridge that gap and take what he so clearly wanted. What she'd so readily asked for. If only the heat between them could be allowed to explode, she'd show him he could be that man again in an instant.

She shook her head and chastised herself silently. Was she never going to learn? This was a business relationship only. Time to get back to that…

"Why would Avery do something so mean? Especially to her own mother."

Jason's head rested against her stomach and his eyes fluttered closed. It was oddly the most intimate moment they'd experienced, as if they were a normal couple helping each other decompress at the end of a long day. It snagged a tender place inside.

For an eternity, she thought he'd fallen into the moment, too, and didn't hear her question.

"Bettina and Avery are like oil and water," he finally said. "Mom says black, Avery says white. Honestly, they were happy to go off to their respective corners when Lynhurst Enterprises split."

"Still." Meredith couldn't quite let go of Jason's broad, strong shoulders and he didn't seem to be in a hurry for her to stop touching him, so she kept up the pressure. "What's a tip-off that turns out to be a lie going to accomplish?"

A ghost of a smile lifted his lips briefly. "It's twofold. Keeps me busy combating the negative press so I'm distracted. And she knows they're not going to uncover anything, but the implications are enough to put Lyn in a bad light. So when she throws in her bid for CEO, she can play up how new management will smooth everything over. Out with the old and in with the new."

"That's…" *Kind of brilliant.* But Meredith didn't dare say it out loud.

"Diabolical and perfect. Plus it upset Mom and that was a great side benefit in Avery's mind."

"But this is only the first strike, right? She'll have more up her sleeve."

The dread Meredith's mother's article had first induced came flooding back. Ferreting out Avery's plans—and hopefully nipping them in the bud—was supposed to be Meredith's job. Fat lot of good she was doing.

"Oh, yeah. This is only the beginning. Now you see why I need you so badly." His voice had turned husky as his muscles relaxed.

She tried to ignore the way the sound tore through her. For a man who wasn't supposed to be her forever, he surely shouldn't cause such strong, involuntary reactions. Especially since he hadn't meant that he needed her the way she wished he had. And she was falling down on the thing he *did* need her for.

"I'm sorry, Jason. This sucks."

She had to do better. Maybe if she succeeded, it would lead to that reconnection she'd been dreaming of.

That thought alone spurred her brain into action, and a half-formed plan began spilling from her mouth. "Here's what we're going to do. Get into a meeting with your marketing department and start brainstorming everything Lyn's done well since the split and then cross-reference that with anything, no matter how small, that Hurst House has stumbled over."

And the subsequent news blast would be titled: Hurst House—Where Is It Now?

Thanks for the article, Mom. Meredith smiled for the first time since last night.

"I'm listening. Then what?"

Meredith massaged his shoulders absently as she worked it over in her mind.

"We're going to bury Hurst House with facts about how fantastic Lyn has done since the split and, by default, how poorly Hurst has fared. We'll pretend the sweatshop witch hunt doesn't exist and by contrast, your rebuttal will come off as a well-written piece of journalism. You and Bettina will be featured as doing a great job, and as a nice side benefit, Avery's going to come out of this looking stupid and petty."

Jason's eyes flew open and he peered up at her. "Whoa. Are you sure you're not a Lynhurst? That's pure genius. It's short only an evil cackle."

Warmth filled her cheeks. Meredith could talk dirty—and then follow through—with the best of them and never think twice about it, yet a *compliment* made her blush? What was the world coming to? "Well, I'll throw the evil cackle in for free."

Jason's appreciative laugh sent the surge of warmth much lower.

"A total bargain." The smile slipped off his face. "Hey. It didn't escape my notice that you said 'we.' You also didn't correct me when I barged in and said we have a problem. You could have easily told me it was *my* problem. Thanks."

Their gazes fused and electricity rippled the atmosphere. *There you are.* Wonderment filled her. *This* was the open, sensitive man she'd left behind in Vegas. Her breath caught. He hadn't vanished and she didn't misremember. Stupid tears of relief pricked at her eyelids and she blinked them away before he noticed.

"Yeah, yeah," she murmured. "We're on the same team. Don't forget it."

"I won't." He reached up and grabbed her hand, bringing it to his lips for a quick kiss. "I wish you could be in the meeting with Marketing. I'd love your insight."

She yanked her tingling hand away from his lips before she forgot about caution and jumped him in hopes of keeping that conduit to his soul open. "Take good notes. Then come back tomorrow night with more takeout and we'll talk."

He grinned. "I've never met a woman who likes to eat as much as you do. It's sexy."

"Shut up and finish your dinner. Serves you right for flirting with me that it's cold," she grumbled and slid into her own chair to finish her own cold dinner.

But it tasted a lot better than it had when it was hot. Because she'd finally seen a glimpse of what she'd hoped for—the man she'd never forgotten.

Now that she'd finally established he was still in there somewhere, how did she keep him around?

Six

Unless the building caved in, Jason's morning couldn't get much worse.

The labor allegations, while complete bunk, grew legs and promised to keep Lyn's entire legal department hopping for the foreseeable future. The fact that the allegations were false didn't seem to matter to Lyn's factory workers, who must have viewed the new development as an opportunity to bring a few choice grievances to upper management. Jason had been funneling complaints to appropriate departments for hours.

Then, his assistant gave her two-week notice. It always sucked to lose critical staff, but she ran his life. He would have doubled her salary if it would have made a difference, but she was marrying her fiancé and moving to Germany.

The meeting with Marketing was nothing short of grueling, but three hours of brainstorming later, the team had an actionable plan. Meredith's idea had put smiles on the faces of his executive staff for the first time today and the press release was nothing short of brilliant.

It was chock-full of shiny highlights about Lyn's progressive fashion lines, one of which was favored by a couple of hot young actresses. Sadly—the release went on to point out—this success sharply contrasted with Hurst's lone lowlight of an evening-wear line that had failed to garner much interest outside of prom shoppers. All of which was true, but the release intentionally left out that the average price tag of a prom dress was fifteen hundred dollars, which contributed greatly to Hurst's bottom line.

A few more carefully selected Lyn Couture hits rounded out the piece, commenting carefully about how the two companies had fared since the split, and the last line contained a pointed message about Lyn's commitment to its workers, particularly those in the Manhattan factory.

Meredith had hit this one out of the park.

By five o'clock, Jason had been at work for over ten hours and fog took over his brain. It was the only reason he couldn't seem to focus on anything except how good Meredith's hands had felt on his tense shoulders last night. Or at least fatigue was his excuse and he was sticking to it.

It had been a nice evening. Casual and expectation free, as it should be. They were basically just friends who'd had a brief affair in the past.

He could get some takeout and drop by her hotel. She'd mentioned as much, so he had the perfect excuse. They could discuss the press release and eat. He didn't have to admit he'd thought about her all day. Or that in unguarded moments, the vivid memories of her body and the way she responded to his touch sneaked into his mind, lacing it with sensual images better suited for a triple-X flick than a boardroom.

Definitely not the thoughts of a friend.

By six, he figured it was late enough that it wouldn't seem as if he was so eager to see her, he'd left work early. He wasn't getting any work done anyway. Traffic wasn't too bad and he arrived at Meredith's hotel quickly.

Meredith swung open the door wearing a button-down oxford with a feminine cut and a pencil skirt. It should have made her look like a schoolteacher but she'd unbuttoned the shirt to the middle of her breasts, allowing the rounded globes to peek out, and the skirt's front-and-center split rose all the way to the juncture of her thighs. One wrong move and she'd show her secrets to the world.

He swallowed as the hard-on he'd been fighting all day raged to life again. The outfit hadn't looked like that on the runway model who'd last worn it at Fashion Week.

Finally his gaze wandered up to Meredith's face, but it was far too late to pretend he hadn't been checking her out. He couldn't have hidden the tenting going on down south, either.

She arched a brow. "You seem to be missing a couple of take-out boxes."

He cursed and fisted his empty hands. "I, uh…forgot."

Her wicked smile punched him in the groin. "Got something else on your mind, then?"

"What makes you say that?" His palms started to sweat. Could she read his thoughts now?

"Oh, I don't know. Because you're here. At my hotel. With no dinner. Kind of made me think you had an interest in an altogether different activity than eating."

Groaning, he scrambled for a response that did not include dipping his tongue into the crevice of her breasts, sliding a hand up the creamy thigh visible beyond the slit of her skirt or silencing her smart mouth with a thorough kiss, which would leave her too breathless to bait him.

He should have left the office at five. At least then he might've still had enough brain cells to remember a simple thing like bringing dinner.

"We should go out." Improvisation at its finest. "That's what I had in mind."

Her laugh tore through the rest of his defenses, weakening his knees.

"Nice recovery," she allowed with a nod. "You and I both know that's not what you were thinking about, but I'll let it slide for now."

Of course she'd realized he was making this up as he

went along. How could he have forgotten how easily she read him? "You're too kind."

Airily, she waved it away. "The sweatshop nastiness was the major topic of conversation at Hurst from morning coffee until quitting time. I'm sure you're exhausted."

"Yeah." He latched on to the handy excuse, which he'd have thought of all by himself if his head was where it should be—on his shoulders and not imagining itself between her thighs. "That's why I'm so absentminded. Work was hellacious."

"Then let's go." She ducked into the room to grab her bag and sling it over her forearm. "I'm dying to hear about the Marketing meeting and anyway, I'm starving. So where are you taking me?"

His response was cut off by a vaguely familiar ringtone emanating from the depths of Meredith's handbag. She fished out her phone and all traces of merriment drained from her face.

"It's Avery," she whispered. "Should I answer?"

"Of course." He crossed his arms as she said hello and listened for a beat.

"Sure. No problem. I'll be there in a few minutes." Meredith stabbed the phone to end the call. "She wants me to come back to the office. It's about her hushity-hush after-hours thingy."

Jason willed back the flood of disappointment. "That's great. Perfect timing."

He'd actually been looking forward to taking Meredith to dinner, never mind that it had originated as a way to save face.

He'd thought seriously about finding some out-of-the-way place and asking for a booth in the back with low lighting, ordering a bottle of wine and spending a couple of hours not thinking about the media circus of Lyn Couture. They'd laugh and flirt and enjoy each other's company. Which sounded an awful lot like a date. That was a bad, bad idea. Avery's timing *was* perfect.

Meredith made a face. "But what about eating?"

"This is more important." *And a far better use of her time.* Lyn and Hurst House were not going to spontaneously regroup, and he'd worked too hard to let what little gains he'd made slip away now. "I'll tell you what. I'll drive you and wait in the car. It can't take more than an hour or so. Then, when you're done, we'll go to a late dinner."

Where had that come from? He should tell her goodnight. But she'd looked so crestfallen, as if she'd experienced a bout of disappointment over Avery's call, as well. He couldn't help himself.

And he was too tired to pretend he didn't want to lose himself in her.

She cocked her head and contemplated him with a small smile. "You'd do that? And here I thought going out was simply an excuse to get us into a public place so I couldn't take advantage of you. If I didn't know better, I'd think you meant the dinner invitation as a date."

"It's not a date," he growled. She definitely had some insight that allowed her to read his thoughts like a book and he did not like it. "And yes, I'll wait for you because I will want you to repeat every word Avery says verbatim. The sooner, the better."

"Of course." She hooked arms with him as they walked to the elevator and bent her head to breathe directly into his ear. "And I'm just here for the clothes."

Jason glanced at his watch, but only three minutes had passed since the last time he'd checked.

What was *taking* so long? Meredith had climbed from his car an hour and a half ago, with a parting squeeze to his thigh that still tingled. He'd tried to work on a strategy brief that needed to go out to the executive staff on Monday, but the only strategy on his mind was Avery's.

His cell phone beeped and he turned it over to see a text from Meredith. With a frown, he tapped it: Avery left and the place is deserted. You've got to come up here and see this.

Craning his neck, he searched the teeming sidewalk for his sister's profile, but he couldn't spot her amid all the foot traffic typical for 9th Street at this time of night. She must have already caught a cab.

What was so important for him to see that Meredith couldn't either tell him about it or take a picture?

He texted her back: What is it?

Meredith: I'm not sure. That's why I need you to look at it.

Jason: You can't just tell me?

Meredith: No, I need you. And I can't disturb the evidence.

And now she'd piqued his curiosity, which probably wasn't an accident.

Did he dare enter the sanctum of his father and Avery? He'd been inside Hurst one time, to attend a meeting nailing down the final details of the split. It had been upsetting to see former Lynhurst employees walking the halls, chatting and laughing as if nothing catastrophic had happened. Then he and Bettina had run into Caozinha Carvalho, the famed photographer who was also his father's new wife, on the way out. His mother had cried in the car on the way back to Lyn.

Before the sun had set, Jason had purchased a plane ticket to Vegas, desperate to get away from the crumbling foundation of his world. Never in a million years would he have guessed the next time he'd contemplate setting foot inside Hurst would be at the invitation of a woman he'd met and married on that trip.

But he was in a different place now, thanks to that woman. And he couldn't resist the opportunity to see inside the company that would be under his command soon. They'd have to avoid the security cameras, but it might be worth the extra care to see what was so important.

Quickly, he texted her back: Meet me at the elevator. I don't have a badge to get past the front doors.

Meredith was waiting for him when the elevator doors split, wearing a cryptic smile. "Thought you'd never get here. Come on."

"Do you know where all the security cameras are?"

"I never paid any attention." Dismay pulled at her expression. "Is it too risky?"

Probably. But he couldn't go back now, not with the dual promise of critical information at his fingertips and a chance to check out his father's company. "I'll keep my face behind my jacket. As long as you're sure no one else is around."

Half-blind, he laced fingers with Meredith, and let her lead him through the quiet office.

When he completed the merger, he planned to let Hurst's space go and rent the floor above Lyn, which would be vacated at the end of the month. He'd already put a deposit down on it in the name of a holding company.

"You and Avery were up here for a long time," he murmured as they passed the door marked *Paul Lynhurst, CEO.*

"Would have been longer if she hadn't gotten another call and hightailed it out of here." Meredith's fingers nested deeper inside his as she turned a corner and pulled him into the office marked *Avery Lynhurst, Vice President of Marketing.*

This was Avery's office? The antique desk and old-world decor did not mesh with the sister he knew, nor did it give the impression cutting-edge fashion happened here. It reminded him of something an eighty-year-old lawyer would prefer.

"So she left you here?" Seemed highly suspicious that Avery would jet with Meredith still in her office, with access to her stuff.

"Oh, no. I walked with her to the elevator, but I'd accidentally-on-purpose forgotten my phone so I shooed her out, insisting I'd be right behind her as soon as I retrieved it." Meredith shrugged mischievously. "It just took a little longer to find my poor lost phone than I expected. Fortunately, she was very eager to get to her next appointment, whatever it was."

When he'd first proposed this plan of planting Meredith in his sister's camp, he'd hoped for a bit of creativity, but this was beyond anything he could have devised. He really owed her.

"I'm very intrigued by the way your mind works." And who would have thought that would be so sexy? He'd long recognized that she had a potent combination of brains and beauty, but this was something else. "Were you always this good at fashion espionage or is this is a new development?"

"Totally new. You've inspired me."

Her smile teased one out of him and he enjoyed it so much, he didn't even care that they were standing there in his sister's office, grinning at each other like idiots—and still holding hands.

"Did you have something to show me?" he prompted.

"Oh, yeah." She dropped his hand and rummaged through some stencils on Avery's desk. "Designs for the new line she's working on. Very secret. Very hot. Very haute couture."

She handed him one and he glanced at it. Instantly, his good humor drained away. "Very stolen, as well."

To his shock, Meredith didn't even blink. She nodded grimly. "I was afraid of that. I didn't think Hurst designed anything like this. It's too high concept. When you first launched Hurst House, what was that, like eight years ago?

Anyway, the line was intended for the rack from the get-go. Accessible designs for real women."

"Yeah, that was the idea. How did you know that?"

"I do my research. When you hooked me up with this job, I wanted to fit in."

"You do," he said shortly. *Too much.* She'd filled a gap he hadn't known existed.

He stared at her with new appreciation. This was why she was so dangerous—he couldn't stay even one step ahead of her.

But all at once, he couldn't remember exactly why that mattered. She felt an awful lot like the solution, not the problem. She'd felt like that in Vegas, too. They'd connected then in a way he'd never connected with anyone. Why had he fought so hard to keep from repeating something so amazing?

"I was right to show these designs to you?" she asked, oblivious to the odd shift going on inside him. "The lines seemed too similar to some of the designs I saw on the walls at Lyn."

"You noticed the *lines* were similar?"

"It's like artwork," she said a touch defensively. "No one would confuse a Van Gogh with a Picasso, right? I thought the designs were suspect."

Captivated, he nodded. She knew style, he'd give her that.

"No, you're right. Hurst doesn't have any designers on staff capable of this kind of work." They certainly didn't have any who were paid to design haute couture. "But it doesn't matter. They were lifted from Lyn's vaults, no question. It's part of our Paris Fashion Week collection. How did Avery get her hands on it?"

They had a spy at Lyn.

He cursed. Avery had stolen his idea to plant a spy *and* stolen Lyn's design.

This was over the top. Sure, Meredith was at Hurst to

gather intel on Avery's CEO plans, but he'd *never* have asked her to steal designs. It was an all-out declaration of war.

Squeal.

Jason froze and Meredith's eyes widened.

Someone was in the hall.

Squeal. Thump.

They were about to get caught in Avery's office.

"It's the janitor," Meredith mouthed. "Quick, get behind the desk."

Pulse thundering, he raised his eyebrows in question.

"Do it," she whispered fiercely and yanked on his arm until he complied.

Kneeling down—and feeling ridiculous—he eyed the crack between Avery's horrendous wooden desk and the floor. The full skirt completely obscured him from view, the only benefit to the heavy furniture. How exactly did it matter if he hid behind the desk while Meredith lounged around plainly in the open?

More squealing emanated from directly outside the office door.

"Good evening," Meredith chirped. "Working late. Do you mind cleaning this office last today? It would be really helpful."

"Sure, miss," a masculine voice responded. The squeals faded into the distance.

Meredith popped around the desk and dusted off her hands. "Piece of cake."

"But he saw you," Jason said over the sudden hum of a vacuum cleaner down the hall.

It should feel even more ridiculous to still be kneeling behind the desk when the imminent danger had passed, but the slit in Meredith's skirt was at eye level and her silky smooth legs kept peeking out, begging for his attention.

And then she shifted and a flash of lacy white seared his vision. His groin went tight and he nearly groaned.

"So?" she asked. "I'm supposed to be here, retrieving my lost phone, remember? If the janitor says anything to anyone, which I doubt he will, that's my excuse. Let's get out of here before he comes back."

That was enough of a reason to stand.

"Good idea." When Meredith picked up the sketches, he shook his head. "Leave them. We don't want her to know we're on to her."

"Okay. But we have to get them back at some point. She can't get away with this."

Meredith's fierce tone made him smile. "If Lyn and Hurst merge, it doesn't matter. I get the designs back by default. No harm, no foul."

It was a lie strictly to soothe her. Avery's treachery hit below the belt and hurt much more than he dared let on.

They sprinted for the elevator and it wasn't until the doors closed that Jason turned to his coconspirator. "That was…"

One glimpse of her made him lose his train of thought.

Meredith's chest rose and fell from the slight exertion, drawing attention to her barely concealed cleavage. Her hair twined around her face in a mess of waves. She was amazing and gorgeous and her quick thinking had saved their hides.

His heart pounded and adrenaline coursed through his veins, waking up his nerves…and drawing the attention of the erection he'd been trying to ignore since the peek at her underwear.

The combination swept over him in a dark surge of awareness, along with a heady dose of her exotic perfume.

Breathing her in, he relaxed and reveled in the wild rush she never failed to evoke. Avery's plans, his plans, mergers, corporate politics—all of it was too much to resolve tonight and he didn't want to think about any of it. Once, he'd fallen into this woman's arms to escape the pain of his real life, and she'd restored him in a way he'd never anticipated.

He craved the connection they'd once had, the one that made him feel as if she understood him in a way no one else could. Why didn't he deserve to have some heat in his otherwise cold life? Why didn't she deserve the same?

Answering awareness sprang into her gaze and her lashes lowered as she focused on his mouth. An instant later, she swayed toward him and their lips fused.

Meredith's essence swept through his senses like a bright white light, clearing away everything but her. She opened under his mouth, her tongue slick against his, so hot and wet and tasting of erotic pleasures. She kissed like she did everything else—with abandon, purpose and raw sensuality. He could not get enough.

Her fingers danced along his spine and threaded through his hair, electrifying his skin wherever she touched. *Meredith*. She made him feel like nothing else ever had or would, as if only he could sate her carnal thirst, as if no other man existed for her.

It was powerful to know a woman like Meredith wanted him. So hot and exciting. Always had been.

Deeper. He plunged his tongue harder, mating with hers, bodies aligned tight. Those magnificent breasts brushed him and he wanted more. He snaked both hands to the small of her back and smashed her breasts against his chest, rubbing against the hardened tips he could feel through their clothes.

He dipped a hand in her skirt, desperate to feel her heated flesh. As he palmed her smooth, taut rear, the elevator doors opened.

Cursing, he tore his mouth from hers and guided her out of the elevator. "Hurry. We're picking up right where we left off."

The faster they reached the car, the less he could question himself about what he was doing. Hell, he already knew where this was going, but he lacked the incentive to stop it. His body screamed for her touch and he wasn't going to say no. Not this time.

He'd worry about angles and leverage and Meredith's odd hold over him tomorrow. Tonight, he wanted to live in the moment and forget about everything else.

Seven

Jason's hand never left Meredith's waist, burning through her clothes with delicious heat. She shivered, nearly stumbling over the curb as he ushered her into the car.

What in the world had gotten into him? If she'd have known a few stolen sketches would bring out his inner Vegas, she'd have scrounged up some long ago.

That kiss had been hot. Like she remembered. Dare she hope this was the start of Amazing, Part II?

"Don't tease me, Jason." She scooted across the backseat of the black town car. "If we're on our way to eat and not my hotel, I'm going to push you out of the car at a very high speed."

The moment he took his seat next to her, he hit the button to raise the panel between the driver and the backseat. The panel whirred, but before it fully nested into place, Jason's mouth was on hers again.

Tipping her head back, he drank from her, tongue tasting her again with the same heat and fervor as he had in the elevator. Well, then. Hotel it was.

She moaned as his mouth rediscovered hers, waves and waves of hot pleasure soaking her with need. Never one to let a man lead, she hiked her skirt up so she could climb into his lap, her lips never leaving his.

Their hips aligned and his hard length rubbed against her core. A long spike of desire tore through her. *Oh, yes, exactly.* She needed this man right now. She rolled her hips, grinding faster, and they groaned in unison.

"Jason," she breathed and nearly came apart at the simple taste of his name on her tongue. A sob rose in her throat and he caught it with another long kiss.

"Right here, baby," he murmured and two fingers slid past the barrier of her panties to explore her damp heat.

Forcefully, he twisted into her, letting her ride his hand as a frisson of white-hot heat flushed over her. Rocking against him faster and faster, she writhed and sparks gathered at the pressure point.

More. Popping the button on her shirt, she palmed her breast and yanked her bra's cup down, offering her nipple to his already-questing mouth. As he sucked it between his teeth and laved the tip with his firm tongue, his thumb circled her nub and that was it.

She came on a thick flood of release, moaning his name and riding the ripples to a finale the likes of which she hadn't experienced in two long years. Slumping against him, she locked her lips against his neck as he stroked two more echoes from her core long past the time she'd expected the climax to end.

"We're here," Jason murmured and withdrew his fingers so sensuously and slowly, her muscles involuntarily clamped down again. "We have to get out."

"Then…stop making me…come."

His wicked laugh put a smile on her face as she reset her clothes. Which didn't take long; Jason was very skilled at finding her sweet spots. Was it any wonder she couldn't move on from a man who made her climax prior to the end of a seven-minute car trip?

He held her hand as he hustled her to the elevator bank. Once in the elevator, he nuzzled her neck, murmuring a few choice phrases about what else he planned to do to her when they got to her room.

Delicious. She just wished she knew what had burst his dam.

It took way too long to reach her floor. They flew from the elevator the moment the doors slid open.

Card key already in hand, he backed her against the door and kissed her thoroughly. She fell into it and into the sensations of the hard planes of his body pressing hers, the wood at her back, the urgency in his hands. All of it stoked a hot flame inside her.

And yet, she hesitated.

She wanted him so badly, but a little worm of doubt wouldn't let her continue until she got some answers, especially the most important one—was all this going to disappear if she blinked?

Pulling back, she put a finger to his beautiful mouth.

"I have to know," she murmured. "What's tonight all about? You've been resistant to this since the moment I walked into your office."

Her hands ached to touch his sculpted abs and her mouth salivated to taste the hard flesh she'd felt pressing into her abdomen. But she didn't move, waiting for his response with bated breath. If he claimed to be acting on the heat of the moment, she'd bid him good-night in a heartbeat. They weren't drunk, and neither of them had a life crisis to blame this on.

This was nothing but two adults coming together because they desperately wanted to be with each other. She needed to know he was choosing this.

"Yes," he acknowledged. "But not because I didn't want you."

"Then why?"

He swayed backward a fraction, but it was enough to alert her she'd hit a nerve. Running a hand through his spiky hair, he released her waist, letting his arm hang at his side. "You've got our experience in Vegas built up in your head as something legendary. I can't maintain that myth for you. I'm just me and you've already expressed disappointment over that."

"Oh, honey." She bit her lip before she spilled too hasty a denial. Because she had said that. "The only reason I have that experience built up in my head is because you're the man who made it legendary. Are you worried it'll only be mediocre?"

Patently ridiculous, if so.

He shook his head. "I'm saying I'm not like I was in Vegas in real life. I don't want to be wild and crazy on a regular basis. I can't. It leads to poor judgment."

As her heart twisted with disappointment, he shifted and pulled her close, wrapping his arms around her so that all the good parts of their bodies aligned. "But you seem to drag my wild side into the light whether I like it or not. I decided to let you, just for tonight."

Had *that* been the golden ticket all along? If she'd seduced him from the get-go, they could have avoided all this drama.

She smiled as her body relaxed in the knowledge that he wasn't about to deny himself what he clearly wanted. Which meant she won, as well. "I see. This is a relationship with an expiration date."

Guess that made it easier for him to let his guard down, as long as he could put it back up in the morning. Or at least that was what he was telling himself. She'd let him think that all he wanted, but that wasn't how it was going to happen.

She stepped aside so he could open the door. Then he picked her up in his strong arms to carry her to the bed, where he laid her out carefully and began unbuckling one stiletto while treating her ankle to butterfly kisses.

She sighed a little. "I thought you didn't believe in romance."

The shoe hit the floor. Eyes half-shut, he rubbed his stubbly jaw over the arch of her foot and murmured, "I said romance was for losers who couldn't get a woman into bed. I didn't need it to get you here. But that doesn't mean I don't think you deserve it."

The back of her throat burned with sudden, unshed tears and she couldn't speak. This was the Jason of two years ago and yet not. He was still gorgeous and pushed all the right buttons, but she didn't remember him being sweet. She couldn't quite get a grip on him.

"Meredith," he said, almost reverently. With extreme care, he took off her other shoe. "You're the most exquisite woman I've ever seen. Bar none. I want to taste you. All over."

"Sounds like a plan to me," she choked out.

"Hope you don't mind if I start here." He slid a hand up her thigh and hooked her panties, drawing them off. Then he parted her skirt at the slit and let his gaze travel over her flesh. He murmured near poetic words of appreciation.

Fevered desire swept along her skin.

He knelt on the bed, gripped her thighs and lowered his head. And then his tongue touched her intimately. Pressing harder, he explored her with the tip and then the broad, rough part laved her. Her eyelids fluttered closed as he pleasured her thoroughly, yanking another climax out of her almost immediately.

She let it wash over her, murmuring his name.

When she recovered, she popped one eye open. "Are you planning to join me at some point? Never mind. You don't have a choice."

While he was busy trying to romance her, she just wanted to put her hands on his naked chest, straddle him and ride into oblivion until they were both spent.

Before he could think of another way to prolong the agony, she jackknifed up from the bed and drew off his suit jacket, tossing it to the floor. Their gazes met and held as she unbuttoned his shirt. A powerful unspoken sense of awareness and electricity passed between them, darkening his expression.

She let the shirt fall from her fingers as his hands tangled in her hair, drawing her head backward so he could nibble at her throat. After what was surely an eternity, she spread her hands on his bare chest, fingertips memorizing the hard muscles.

"I want all of you," she murmured and quickly divested him of the remainder of his clothes, while he peeled her out of the outfit he'd given her.

When he was gloriously bare, she indulged herself in a good, long perusal. Mouth slightly quirked up, he stood still as she soaked in the perfection of Jason's body, especially the jutting arousal that signified how much he wanted her.

It was a thing of beauty.

And she wanted to make him feel as good as he'd made her feel. Kneeling before him, she ran her tongue along his hard shaft until she felt his fingers grip the back of her head. Instantly, she remembered that meant he was ready for more. So she drew him into her mouth and sucked until he pulsed against her tongue.

Harder and harder she sucked until he groaned and locked his knees, then came in a rush that left her feeling wickedly powerful.

"And now for the main course," she announced and backed him up to the bed where he collapsed in a heap, groaning her name. "Wait here."

She dashed to the bathroom to clean up and retrieve a dozen condoms—because if history was any indication, they'd need them all.

When she returned to the bed, he hadn't moved, as instructed. He lay there, arm over his eyes, clearly recovering from the massive orgasm she'd given him.

Shamelessly, she climbed up the length of his body to kiss him soundly. "Miss me?"

The arm moved and his dark gaze fastened on hers.

"Much more than I should have. You weren't gone that long."

Oh, my. There he went being sweet again. She'd mostly been kidding. What was he trying to do to her? "Here I am."

She squealed when he flipped her under him, and then his tongue was in her mouth, so she wisely let him kiss her senseless. All vestiges of humor drained away as his hands caressed her, taking her deep under his spell. The world fell away and became nothing more than a sea of sensation. When he lifted his head, breaking the long kiss, she whimpered.

"Just a sec," he whispered and sheathed himself one-handed, then parted her thighs.

Yes, oh, yes. She thrust upward as he entered her and they joined completely, inch by delicious inch.

Wrapping her legs around him so he couldn't move, she cupped his jaw and just looked at him for a moment. His heated gaze locked with hers. The moment stretched, filling her with the strangest sense of awe.

Jason was here. He was with her, inside her, surrounding her. Her heart shifted and resettled and finally felt as if it was in the right place. She almost cried out with the perfection of it. Only at that moment did she realize the sharp pieces of her fractured soul had been digging into her for two years. And in one instant, Jason had healed her.

"Make love to me," she whispered.

Oh, no. She'd said that out loud.

They'd never made love before. They'd had plenty of hot, dirty sex. But that had been before she went without him for two years.

She liked hot, dirty sex, like the fully clothed orgasm she'd had in the car while throngs of people raced around them, oblivious to the couple getting it on inside. Sex was part of her due as a human being, and she'd always made sure to get plenty of it. All at once, she wanted something more.

And it scared her. Making love wasn't what she and Jason did. He wanted wild and crazy, like they'd had in Vegas, for one night. He liked that she brought out that side of him, which wouldn't happen if she got all maudlin.

Besides, this was a relationship with an expiration date and they'd both agreed to that. For crying out loud, they were days away from signing divorce papers. What had gotten into her?

Clamping down on all the emotions, she smiled wickedly as he stared down at her, clearly at a loss about what she was asking for.

"But not like this," she said and flexed one hip to roll him off her. Fortunately, he let her because there was no way she could have moved a man his size with her own strength alone. Then she slung a leg over his waist.

Astride his muscular frame now, she placed both palms on his chest, like she'd been fantasizing about for days. Years. "Much better."

She began to move and flung her head back to keep him from seeing anything extra in her eyes that she didn't want to reveal.

Pure pleasure. Nothing wrong with that.

And pleasure her he did. Jason reached up to cup her breasts as she found her rhythm, tweaking her nipples expertly. Losing herself in him wasn't hard.

He groaned. "I love your body. It's the hottest I've ever seen, even in airbrushed magazines."

"And it's all yours, for now," she teased and pretended the catch in her throat was due to the physical pleasure instead of how sad "for now" had suddenly made her. What was *wrong* with her?

Hot. Dirty. Wild. Crazy. These were the things she should be focusing on. She threw herself into it, abandoning her thoughts to the heat Jason had created. His hips matched her thrusts, spiraling her into the heavens in another climax.

She slumped onto his chest, resting her cheek against his thundering heart. His arms held her tight and she shut her eyes. But she couldn't go to sleep cradled by this man like she desperately wanted to. It meant something different now than it had in Vegas.

She'd made the monumentally earth-shattering discovery that when she'd dreamed of reconnecting with Jason Lynhurst, it hadn't been about sex. Not solely. Maybe it hadn't even been just sex in Vegas, but she'd never stopped to examine it.

Her heart hurt and not in a good way. Was all this why she'd gotten so teary over his simple romantic gestures earlier? Why she couldn't forget him? All she'd wanted was a taste of his magic again, the feel of his body and the rush of a release only he seemed capable of giving her.

And he had. What else could she possibly ask for? Once she had the divorce, she could move on, go home and become a successful businesswoman. That's what the Grown-Up Pact was about, what she wanted. Didn't she? Frustrated, she bit her lip. This emotional muddle was not on the agenda.

After a few minutes of struggling to hold back the flood of confusion inside, she finally thought she could speak without tipping him off that she'd experienced a total freak-out. "You've still got the moves, sugar. Anytime you want wild and crazy, you let me know. I'm your girl."

"I'll keep that in mind." He kissed her on the temple and spooned her against him. "Do you want me to stay?"

Of course she did. But coupled with the swirl of uncertainty and the fact that he'd actually asked made her blurt out, "You don't have to."

And then she hoped he'd see right through her words and insist that he wanted to stay. But he nodded and rolled away, taking his heat with him. "I do have an early meeting."

She smiled and faked being okay with him jetting off in the middle of her crisis. After all, she'd given him permission to leave. This wasn't a vacation where they could lounge around in bed for a whole weekend. He was busy. So was she. "See you later."

Actually it was better if he went, for both of them. This is what adults did when having a short-term affair. It was what *she* did. Always.

She didn't watch him get dressed and didn't glance up when she heard him turn the doorknob to leave. It was cold in this icebox of a hotel room. She pulled the blanket up to cover herself.

Long after he left, she stared at the wall, wondering how in the world they'd managed to get naked and have cataclysmic orgasms and yet she hadn't gotten what she wanted at all.

Eight

With something akin to a herculean effort, Jason managed to hit the threshold of his office by eight o'clock. How, he had no idea. He'd tossed and turned all night, only to fall asleep at 5:00 a.m., thirty minutes before his alarm.

If only he could blame the inability to sleep on Avery's thievery or the merger plans or the damaging press he had been combating. As bad as all that was, it couldn't hold a candle to the vision of Meredith on permanent repeat in his head.

Oddly, the memory wasn't of her naked—though she had the body of any breathing man's wet dream. No, the image haunting him was of her in the car, when she'd mounted him with that little skirt hiked up and her breasts half spilling from her clothing.

The look on her face...rapturous. He couldn't stop watching her as he pleasured her. Sure, he'd been touching her intimately while in public, which was the very definition of the kind of crazy she induced. He should have been appalled at himself. Instead, he'd felt alive, invigorated. Powerful in the knowledge that he could make her come as many times as he wanted and she'd cry out *his* name.

That's why he hadn't stayed. Because he'd liked reconnecting with her far too much.

He groaned and groped blindly for the fresh cup of coffee on his desk, gulping it in hopes of banishing his wicked vixen of a wife from his mind. The coffee scalded his tongue and he swore. Colorfully.

There was not enough coffee in all of Midtown Manhattan to caffeinate him well enough to face the day anyway. He dumped the whole cup in the trash. Might as well make his morning complete by calling Avery.

Anyone who would steal a company's bread and butter deserved a special place in hell.

When Avery answered on the first ring, he knew something was up and the back of his neck tingled. "Hey. We need to talk."

How to bring up the designs? If he dove right into an accusation, Avery would figure out how to weasel out of admitting anything. Maybe he'd get the lay of the land first and then work his way up to it.

"I agree," she said smoothly. "I've been talking to Paul about the points made in the oh-so-clever article you released. By the way, nice job with that, little brother."

The sarcasm was so thick, he grinned. Meredith's strategy had worked. That article must have really pissed off Avery for her to be so nasty right out of the gate. "Marketing, plain and simple. Surely you of all people appreciate the value of truth in advertising."

She paused long enough for Jason to wonder if the connection had been lost.

"I'm a fan of the truth, actually," she returned cryptically. "So I mentioned to Paul that you weren't off the mark. Hurst doesn't have the heavy hitting haute couture reputation of Lyn. It's not in our DNA, nor our strategy. If we want to run with the big dogs, we have to consider our weaknesses."

Ah. So that was the reason behind the stolen designs. She planned to use them to launch a line that would compete with Lyn. But surely she realized that at least twenty people could attest under oath that those designs had originated inside Lyn's walls, not to mention the digital footprint of the saved files with date/time stamps. Hurst's reputation wouldn't be haute couture *or* prom dresses—it would become famous for being a company full of convicted felons.

The whole concept made him a little sick.

"What did Paul say?" Uttering his father's name didn't help the queasiness.

"This and that," she hedged. "The important thing is that I laid the foundation for the merger. So in reality, our dueling media blitz only helped that cause." And that would be the only admission he'd ever get that she'd orchestrated the sweatshop allegations. "In a few days, I'm going to mention the need for a new strategy. Then I'll casually drop the hint—have you thought about the benefits of bringing the company back under one roof?"

God, she was good. If he hadn't known about the stolen designs, he might have actually bought that song and dance. Avery didn't have a problem playing both sides of the table, obviously. And neither did he.

Suddenly, he didn't see the value in mentioning the designs. He'd rather wait to see how that played out. Though he'd still have to find a way to deal with the spy in his company.

"Fantastic. I'll do the same with Bettina, though I'll focus on revenue. She's interested in launching a swimsuit line." Normally, he wouldn't mention detail, but with it on the table, Avery couldn't steal it out from under Bettina now. "It would be a good time to talk financing and how expensive new lines are. Hurst's numbers are better than they've ever been, according to what you've told me. That's still true, right?"

"Of course." She sniffed. "Hurst House is and always will be the cash cow of the Lynhurst empire."

"This is great," he said heartily. "It's progress, which is sorely needed. Now we have to work on how to convince Paul and Bettina to relinquish their CEO roles to us."

The hope was that they could figure out a way to make

it seem attractive to retire or find other projects. Paul was going to be difficult as he'd been on the business side since the inception of Lynhurst Enterprises, whereas Bettina was a designer at heart. It might be possible to get her interested in stepping aside.

As always, Jason cared more about Bettina's feelings than Paul's. Honestly, if Jason and Avery ended up doing a hostile takeover of Hurst, it would be exactly what his father deserved.

After all, it was Paul's fault the company had split. And Paul's fault Hurst and Lyn weren't doing as well separately as they'd done together. But a hostile takeover would be difficult and costly and would breed ill will. It would be better to avoid it if possible.

"It's a problem," Avery conceded. "We'll have to brainstorm on how to solve it."

Inspiration hit, brought on solely by the combination of Meredith calling him up to Hurst's office and the night of passion following. "When you're hinting around about the merger, mention to Paul that he might want to take a backseat role in order to spend more time with Caozinha."

It was the first time he'd ever called his father's wife by her name. Since he didn't immediately feel like rinsing out his mouth with Jack Daniel's, he'd call that a victory.

"That'll work." Faint praise, but from Avery, it was practically the same thing as a gold medal.

They talked a few more minutes about some of the merger's legal details and when Jason hung up, he had to chalk it up to one of the more pleasant conversations he'd had with his sister in quite some time.

Either knowing about her secret plans had mellowed him or Meredith had. Maybe each had had an effect. And his wife was responsible for both. Who would have thought he'd gain such a valuable asset when he'd come to Meredith with the idea of not signing the divorce papers right away?

Mood vastly improved, Jason put the hammer down on

his to-do list and, by eleven, managed to accomplish more than he'd have expected. Which was fortunate because two minutes later, Meredith texted him: Meet me at the hotel for lunch. I have an idea.

Instantly, his mind filled in that blank. He had an idea, too. Several, in fact. Already happily anticipating another skipped meal, he texted her back: I'm walking out the door.

He canceled his one o'clock meeting and caught himself humming by the time he hit the elevator. Looked as if he wasn't against wild and crazy in the middle of the day, either.

Meredith was already in the room when he pushed the door open. God, she was exquisite, with silky hair halfway down her back. Her beautiful face—he could stare at it for hours.

"That was fast," she commented over her shoulder as she bent over the desk scribbling something on the phone pad. "Give me a minute."

"You take all the time you need." Because she was precisely where he wanted her.

He came up behind her and put both hands at her waist, fitting that shapely rear against his already-aching groin. The filmy sundress she wore scarcely provided a barrier and he could feel the folds of her sex. Hard as steel, he rubbed her intimately, pleasuring them both.

She stilled and then shifted, deliberately sliding against his erection.

"Oh, so that's how it's going to be?" she asked, her voice hitching.

"Uh-huh," he murmured and gathered her hair in one hand, holding it away from her neck. He nibbled at the creamy flesh revealed, grinding into her deeper.

Oh, yeah. So sweet.

She reached back and yanked the hem of her dress up to her waist, then guided his free hand to one breast. "If you're going to do it, do it right, honey." She arched backward, thrusting her hips in powerful bursts.

He nearly came then, still fully clothed, but he fought it long enough to thumb down the neckline of her dress, spilling her breast into his palm. Groaning, he took the nipple between his fingertips and the hot flesh pebbled instantly.

"I want to be inside you," he mouthed against her neck as he kissed it from behind.

"Condoms are in the bathroom. I'm not going anywhere."

He peeled away from her with no small effort and dashed to grab the string of foil packets lying on the vanity.

When he returned to the main area, Meredith stood palms-down at the desk, skirt still flipped up over her back. But she'd kicked off her panties and spread her legs in invitation. She turned her head a fraction and peered up at him through a curtain of hair. Her expression said he better hurry because she was impatient.

It was the single most erotic thing he'd ever seen. Dark, wicked lust zigzagged through his midsection.

His fingers shook as he tore off his pants and rolled on a condom over the fiercest erection he'd ever experienced. In seconds, he was back in place against her, gripping her hips and sliding into her heat.

She closed around him and the exquisite pressure heightened the urgency. He needed her. He reached for her nub, cradling her against his torso as he fingered her, driving them together again and again until she cried out. Her release squeezed him so perfectly that he followed her instantly. Eyes closed and lips against her neck, he let the orgasm blast through him.

Chest heaving with the exertion, he slapped a hand next to hers on the desk, bracing himself so he didn't collapse on her. "That was…"

Amazing. Unbelievable. But those words were so cliché for what she made him feel.

"Hot and dirty?" she suggested.

"And then some." They'd had sex in many inventive lo-cations and positions before, but never in the middle of a workday when they both had to go back to an office. Some-how, the spontaneity had heightened the pleasure. And now he wanted her all over again.

He separated their bodies and turned her in his arms to lay a kiss on her lips. But as he started to lower his head, their gazes caught, freezing him. Vulnerability and ten-derness flickered through her expression and he couldn't look away. One strap of her sundress fell off her shoulder and he slid it back into place, resting his hand on her still-hot flesh in a moment of perfect harmony that rocked him to the core.

All at once, he remembered similar moments from Vegas. After coming down from the height of their cli-maxes, they'd roll together and hold each other. Then they'd whisper things in the dark, secret things, fears. Hopes. Dreams. It had made the whole experience of sex some-thing otherworldly. It was in those moments that she'd given him peace.

And nothing had changed.

When he'd given in to his desire for Meredith, he hadn't gotten just the wild and crazy he'd asked for. Maybe that wasn't all he'd been looking for, either, despite the lies he seemed willing to tell himself. He needed *her*, if only to remind himself that he wasn't cold-blooded. With her, he could be a man he actually liked.

"Meredith," he murmured and drew her forward into the kiss he suddenly ached for. Her lips molded to his, and she snuggled into his embrace. It was comfortable and sexy and right.

As he angled her head to take them both deeper, she pulled away and cleared her throat. "You know, normally a guy starts out with the kiss, but it's fine if you want to do it the other way around."

Gaze on the floor, she located her panties and disappeared into the bathroom as if he wasn't standing there. At a loss, he drew his own clothes back on and pulled out his phone to check his email because it felt less pathetic than following her into the bathroom to demand an explanation for why she'd cooled down so fast.

She didn't owe him peace. He certainly hadn't given her any.

When she returned, the temperature hadn't risen much.

"So about my idea," she began and perched on the edge of the desk where they'd just had hot and dirty sex, as she'd dubbed it.

"That wasn't your idea?" He nodded to the scene of the crime.

"Uh, no. That was totally your idea."

Frowning, he searched her blank expression. "You seemed pretty on board with it."

"Of course I was." Impatiently, she flipped a lock of hair behind her back. "You're the sexiest man I've ever met. You pretty much just have to breathe on me to get me hot. But it wasn't what I had in mind when I texted you. The condoms were in the bathroom after all, not on the desk."

The compliment sounded decidedly uncomplimentary somehow. "Funny, I've been thinking about you all day."

"You wanna know what I've been thinking about? How to get the designs back from Avery." The fierce scowl on her face piqued his ire in kind because he had no idea what had set her off. "And I have an idea how to accomplish that. If you'll get your brain out of my panties, we can talk about it."

"That's rich, Meredith. You've been very free with the invitations into your panties, starting from second one in my office. Don't act like I'm the only horny one."

The oasis of peace vanished so fast, he wondered if he'd imagined it.

"What should I act like, then? Your wife?" She sneered.

"Because that's what I'm trying to do here. Give you what you want out of this marriage so we can both be done with it."

His hands fisted at his sides as pure frustration threatened the careful grip he held on his temper. "Why are you picking a fight with me?"

"Because! I..." She deflated all at once and sank into one of the chairs at the table, her head down. After a beat, she said, "I'm not trying to pick a fight. I just want to do my job and go home. Can you give me a break, here? I need you to understand. I have to go home."

Her gaze met his and all his mad drained away, as well. This conversation was upsetting her. But why? Did she want to get away from him that badly?

Clearly. And could he blame her? He'd held her up for an extra week already. She had a real life to get back to, just like he did. Obviously she didn't crave a warm place at his side, where together they could combat the cold, harsh business of daily life.

"Tell me your idea," he said, crossing to her and taking her hand so she could sense his sincerity. And because he wanted to touch her. "Really. If it works and I get the designs back, I'll call it even."

"Even?"

Her fingers curled around his. It was enough of a truce to force him to spit out the clarification—even though he didn't want to. He owed her and she deserved what she'd earned.

"I'll sign the papers." He swallowed against the sudden burn in his throat. Too late to take it back now. "I'll get my lawyer to expedite the divorce, and you can be on a plane before you know it. First class, my treat. How's that for understanding?"

It was yet another lie. In reality, he didn't understand at all. Because he didn't want to let her go and it had nothing to do with leverage or sex or anything he could name.

* * *

Meredith blinked. "Just like that?"

It was almost over. She could go back to Houston, divorce in hand, and start figuring out how to scrub Jason from her soul. The faster she got away, the easier it would be to sort out all the confused feelings she couldn't seem to untangle.

Obviously, he was just as eager to get rid of her. Last night he'd insisted this relationship had an expiration date, which she'd conveniently ignored.

That had been before she'd realized sex and their affinity and all the things she'd dreamed about for two years were somehow connected via her heart.

"Sure." He shrugged nonchalantly as if it didn't matter either way. "Once I have the designs back, what else could you do? You've succeeded at exactly what I asked for. I've got intel on Avery's plans, and the information is stellar. Better than I could have hoped."

Jason was conceding. He'd given her high praise and told her she'd nearly fulfilled the terms he'd laid out. The elation should be so great, she shouldn't be able to hold it back. Instead, she felt as if she couldn't breathe.

"So you want me to do this one last thing and then I'm done?"

He nodded. "Seems like that's what I'm saying."

Fantastic. The timing couldn't be better. She didn't know how much longer she could keep being Jason's wild and crazy go-to girl. Not when the entire time he'd been blowing her mind against the desk she'd been so very aware that she wanted more, wanted him like he was during their stolen moments, but permanently. And she had a hard time not demanding it from him.

For once in her life, she was going to act like an adult and sleep in the bed she'd made. Which wasn't Jason's. He didn't want anything more than sex and honestly, that's all he'd wanted in Vegas, too. It was all *she'd* wanted…until she didn't.

How was she supposed to know that sex would create a deluge of emotions? Or that she'd have no idea how to handle them? That was her own fault, not his, and it wasn't fair to demand anything of him other than a divorce, especially when she was clueless about what she'd even demand.

Squaring her shoulders, she nodded once. "Awesome. So Avery has a meeting next week with some people about the after-hours project. I don't know what it's about, but I do know that Paul is on her case about the bad juju you created with the press release."

It had given her a thrill to know she'd had a hand in the tightness around Avery's mouth. The whole office had been walking on eggshells all morning and doing their level best to stay out of Avery's way. Except Meredith. She'd walked straight into the lion's den and volunteered to help.

No one had to know she'd done it for Jason as much as she'd done it for the divorce.

"She told me," Jason offered. "They're trying to do damage control with a strategic move. I think the stolen designs became a part of it."

Avery hadn't shared anything that detailed with Meredith. "I didn't realize you'd spoken to her."

He raised his eyebrows endearingly. "Didn't I mention it? Oh, that's right. I was a little busy with the desk gymnastics and then wading through the fight that wasn't a fight."

The eye roll she shot him wasn't nearly sarcastic enough. "*I've* been trying to have this conversation for forty-five minutes now. *You* started the desk gymnastics."

"You were the one bent over the desk wearing that sexy little dress. Next time, sit down. Or wear a potato sack."

His teasing tone saddened her a little.

If only things hadn't gotten so complicated, she'd probably have flashed her nipples in deliberate provocation, hoping he'd get her naked again. But the fact that he saw

nothing wrong with flirting in the same breath as inform-
ing her she could go home told her everything she needed
to know. She'd made the right decision to keep her mouth
shut about what was going on inside her.

"So anyway." She drew the last word out lightly, but
they needed to get back on topic before she fell apart. "A
drumroll would be a little anticlimactic at this point, but
I'm going to ask Avery to let me take her place at this
meeting about the after-hours project so she can focus on
Paul's strategy concerns. She might say no, but it's worth
it to ask."

"I'm impressed." Jason crossed his arms and leaned
against the wall, the same spot he'd been in since she returned from the bathroom. "It's a good idea and I like it.
When is the meeting?"

"I think it's Monday." Which meant she had the rest of
the afternoon to work out how she'd get Avery to agree.
It was all in the timing, especially if she could corner the
busy woman right after the two-hour meeting Avery had
booked with Paul Lynhurst later today.

Surely that meeting would end with a number of action
items assigned to Avery with no relief in sight. Meredith,
to the rescue.

And if Avery didn't want Meredith to know her sched-
ule, she shouldn't leave her calendar open on her phone in
plain sight.

"Will she go for it?" Jason asked. "Avery doesn't trust
anyone. Have you gotten close enough to her that she'd give
you such an important task?"

Meredith shrugged. "Can't hurt to try. But it's the only
shot I'll have to get the designs into my possession without
raising her suspicions and then oops. Maybe I accidentally
set them on fire. You have backup files, right?"

"You bet."

"And if I get lucky, she'll fire me. I'll be going home
soon anyway, so it's a chance to tell her what I really think

of her. It will probably include swearing." Judging by the way Jason's grin widened, her plan met with his approval. "So you're cool with all this? Without the designs, she has no strategy left and you'll be able to expose her as a thief. We're talking about ruining Hurst. A company run by your father and your sister. No second thoughts?"

"My father ruined Hurst all on his own when he split it apart," Jason countered fiercely. "Whatever he gets is no less than he deserves."

His entire demeanor changed in a snap. Distress warred with passion, and his body fairly vibrated with it. His vitality bled through the atmosphere to ping around inside her.

Open, vulnerable Jason from Vegas hadn't grown up and grown cold—he'd transferred his angst and helplessness into his merger plans. How had she missed that? He'd talked about his plans before—a lot—but always in a factual kind of way.

This was different. He'd never revealed so much in so few words, especially not about his feelings toward his father.

"Tell me about it," she commanded softly, terrified she'd shove him back behind his walls if she pushed too hard. But if she could bring out the wild and crazy in him, surely she could coax out more of the sensitive and passionate, as well. She had to try.

Intimacy and soul-baring conversations—it was the stuff of her fantasies. If she'd begged him to stay last night, could they have gotten there then?

He took a deep breath, clearly struggling to maintain his composure.

"That's why it's so important for me to reunite Lyn. I'm going to fix it. Paul failed, as a father, as a husband, as a CEO." Jason's hands fisted at his sides, his mouth twisting into a frown. "My mom never wanted to be in management. But he forced her into it when he left."

His ravaged expression nearly undid her.

She ached for him and for his mother. Avery, too, as at least some of her abrasive personality probably stemmed from her hurt over the events of two years ago. Meredith had a lot of sympathy for them all. "I'm sorry, honey."

"Don't be. I'm going to step up and be the man he wasn't. I'm going to make the company whole again, and if I'm CEO, then he can't be. It's the perfect payback for what he did to Lynhurst Enterprises because running things was always his role."

"Oh, honey." She shook her head and let a small smile bloom. "You might be telling yourself that this is all about revenge, but admit it. You're working so hard on this merger for your mom."

Surprise flitted across his expression. Had he not realized that until this moment?

"I'll give you that one. It's partially true. I forget how easily you read me," he groused but didn't seem too upset about it.

He'd designed his dastardly plans to right the wrongs his father had done to his mother. It was somehow sweet and her heart squeezed with raw emotion. Unable to stop herself, she slid from the chair and wrapped him in a tender embrace.

"You look like you need a hug," she offered in explanation, though he hadn't asked and it wasn't exactly true.

She needed the contact, needed to touch this complex, wonderful man buried underneath the fashion-espionage mastermind.

His arms encircled her, holding her tight, and he rested his head on top of hers.

They stood there wrapped in each other and it was every bit the connection she'd yearned for. And they were both fully dressed. Who would have seen that coming?

"I have to get back to work," Jason said gruffly. "It's really late."

"Yeah."

Lots of work to do this afternoon. Lots of Allo to endure and lots of Avery to outwit. The thought exhausted her all of a sudden. All she really wanted to do was stay in the circle of Jason's arms for the next week or two and forget about real life.

Since that wasn't in the master plan, she stepped back and shoved him lightly. "Go. But come back. Bring dinner and I'll tell you about my conversation with Avery."

They weren't divorced yet. Until then, she'd keep pushing for that connection.

Nine

There was literally no point in Jason going back to work if he intended to get anything done. Apparently, taking a two-hour lunch meant an afternoon of interruptions.

An interview had surfaced in the press sometime in the past few hours with more sweatshop allegations, this time from an unnamed source who claimed to be a current Lyn employee. It was not pretty. And he had the worst feeling Avery wasn't behind this one, which meant he had bigger problems.

When Bettina pinged Jason via instant message asking him to come to her office, he groaned. He could not deal with another round of his mother's teary, mournful snuffling over the continued media onslaught. Yes, they were maligning the company with her name on it, but it was his name, too, and if she wanted him to fix it, she needed to give him a break.

It was shaping up to be a late night at the office. There went his plans for takeout with Meredith, which he'd been actively anticipating.

"This is the last time, Mom," he muttered to his laptop screen and grabbed a Red Bull from the small refrigerator by his desk for fortification.

When had he turned into such a liar? He'd be there for his mother forty-seven more times today if that's what she needed. When Paul moved out two years ago, Jason had been his mother's only ally. Gladly. After all she'd done for Jason, it was the least he could do for her. Plus, she was his mom.

Chugging the energy drink, he poked his head into Bettina's office and she was smiling.

"There you are. Come in," she invited and leaped up from behind her desk, rounding it more quickly than a sixty-year-old woman should be able to.

Before Jason could blink, she'd thrown her arms around him in a totally out-of-character motherly hug. He hugged her back, mystified by what had prompted such a turnabout.

"Avery told me," his mother said when she stepped back to look at him with a misty smile. "Though why you didn't, I'll never understand."

"Told you what?" Baffled, he searched his mother's expression for some clue as to what had elevated her mood.

"About the wife you've been hiding from everyone."

"About the...*what*?" Jason's stomach tensed as his mother came in for another round of hugs.

Should he brazen it out or come clean? Well, obviously it was too late to pretend he didn't know what Bettina was talking about.

Avery. He swore. He'd underestimated her yet again. How had she found out? God, this was so much worse than labor allegations. He should have seen this coming.

"Why didn't you tell me you'd gotten married?" his mother scolded, but the thrill in her voice belied the reprimand.

"Uh...I thought you'd be upset." Since that clearly wasn't the case, he scrambled for how to spin this new development, while simultaneously trying to figure out why Avery had struck at him in this particular way.

"On the contrary. It's the best news I've had in a long time." Her voice lowered. "I would never have said anything, but I didn't like the idea of you marrying Meiling in some kind of loveless arrangement. But a whirlwind romance and quick wedding? That's wonderful."

"I'm glad someone thinks so," he mumbled darkly.

He'd assumed Bettina would see the business benefits of his "arrangement" with Meiling. Fine time to find out differently.

His mother clapped her hands. "You must let me take you and your wife to dinner so I can meet her. Avery said she's working at Hurst? Which I don't understand, but I'm sure you can explain."

He muttered another curse under his breath and shut his eyes. Bettina's feelings were hurt that he'd let his wife work for The Enemy.

Jason was going to kill Avery. Slowly. "It's complicated."

She nodded, growing serious. "With your father and I on such bad terms, how could it be anything but? The divorce was hard on all of us. But you don't have to hide the most important relationship of your life from me. Sure I'm lonely occasionally, but that doesn't mean I don't wish great things for you. I'm genuinely happy that you've found someone."

Oh, man. Bettina thought he hadn't told her out of fear she'd be *jealous*? That wasn't precisely the sort of "upset" he'd assumed she'd be if she discovered he'd married Meredith in front of an Elvis impersonator in Vegas, while intoxicated. Two years ago, no less.

The Lyn and Hurst executive staffs wouldn't see his Vegas wedding as a plus, and Avery probably had more fun surprises in store for him regarding when and how she'd drop this marriage bombshell to others.

Damage control needed, ASAP.

"Thanks, Mom," he interjected smoothly. "And for the record, Meredith is only working at Hurst temporarily. I'm sorry I didn't tell you she was my wife when I asked you for the recommendation."

At least he didn't have to lie to preserve his mother's feelings. He wasn't hiding Meredith from Bettina by placing her at Hurst. But she needed to understand that his marriage wasn't going to last much longer. *Before* she started naming her imaginary grandchildren.

He had a feeling this news was not going to go over well. Bettina would be very disappointed that her son wasn't happily married after all. How had he gotten to this place?

"Mom, Meredith and I, we're not—"

"Oh, don't say you're not interested in dinner. I'm dying to meet my new daughter-in-law. I want to hear all the wedding details. And you're really horrible for not taking her on an extended honeymoon. Be sure you make that up to her."

New daughter-in-law? Was it possible Avery didn't actually spill the whole story? Or even better, perhaps Avery didn't actually know the full story. There was still a possibility of salvaging this situation. "Please, Mom. I do not now, nor do I ever, want you to explain what you think I should do to make it up to her."

Bettina laughed. "Let me take you to dinner. Are you free tonight?"

"We had plans to get takeout."

"Then it's settled." She leaned in and took Jason's hand in hers. His mother's skin felt paper-thin and prominent veins stood out against her wrinkles. When had she aged so much? "I worry about you. I'm glad you decided to settle down and spend your life with someone. It makes it so much easier to think about retiring."

"Retiring?"

That word had never come out of Bettina's mouth. His mother was one of the biggest obstacles to his plans because she'd never approve of merging with Hurst. He'd been racking his brain for a way to convince her to focus on her new swimsuit line and let him take care of the company.

But if Bettina retired…it was a whole new game.

Bettina patted his hand. "Not today. But maybe soon. I

didn't want to consider retiring, but now that you're settled, I can leave Lyn in your hands with confidence."

Settled. It had a much nicer ring than he'd have anticipated. Jason's gut spasmed at the same moment his mind spun in a billion directions. *What if he didn't have to end things with Meredith so quickly?*

Instantly, Jason's vision of the future shifted. He could stay married. And he had the perfect excuse to avoid examining why that was such a great thing.

"You'll be a fantastic CEO," Bettina finished with a nod.

Right. That's what he should be focusing on, not Meredith and her special ability to drive him insane. His mother was talking about retiring and naming him as the next CEO, a huge win for his plans.

If he was already the CEO of Lyn, the merger would go a lot more smoothly, and no one would question whether he should continue to be the head of the newly reformed company.

Because he would be *married.* To Meredith.

Who wanted a divorce, which he'd conveniently forgotten.

In the mixed-up, crazy place Jason's life had become, the wife he'd been working to get rid of was now the wife he apparently needed to keep. His marriage had just become very valuable.

Marriage was a tool. He'd always thought so. This was nothing new, nothing different. Meredith knew this and all he needed to do was have a conversation with her about the change of plans. She'd handle the curveball, despite the fact that he'd told her a few hours ago he'd sign the papers.

His palms started to sweat. "I have to get back to work. I'll let you know about dinner."

Bettina's glowing smile stuck with him the rest of the afternoon. As did the cramp in his stomach. He couldn't sign the papers, not even if Meredith got the designs back. And he had the worst feeling she'd hear the phrase "no divorce" and it would paint him as ruthless and cold-blooded…and exactly like Avery.

At which point she'd likely express her disappointment again over who he'd become. And then he'd have to think about how he longed to be a better man, the one she encouraged him to be.

Actually, as soon as he mentioned staying married a little while longer, she'd probably smile and say something provocative about him using this as an excuse to get her into his bed.

God, he hadn't thought that far ahead. But it only made sense that she had to move into his house, didn't it? That's what married people did. And how dumb would it be to suggest she stay in his guest room? But if he suggested she sleep with him, what did that imply?

Obviously, it implied he was asking her to move in with him and be his wife. In every sense. Because he wanted to be around her, live with her, sleep with her, like they were in a relationship. Something hitched in his chest as he imagined waking up next to Meredith every morning, her gaze sleepy and full of promise.

Yes. That's what he wanted.

No. He couldn't let her think that. There was no way he'd ever have a marriage based on anything other than how it could help him further his merger plans. People who fell in love eventually fell out of love and damaged everything around them, and he'd never willingly do that to anyone.

Nor could he give her the impression this was a desperate ploy to get a few more days with her, though he liked that aspect of it more than he should. If only this had happened before they'd started sleeping together again, the complications would be far fewer. And he'd never have to admit, not even to himself, that he wanted to seize this opportunity to keep her around.

Fortunately, he and Meredith saw eye to eye on the purpose of their marriage.

Meredith was starving and Jason had taken his sweet time getting to her hotel after work.

He finally knocked at ten after seven.

The darkness in Jason's gaze had her immediately itching to smooth the line from between his eyes. Tension was evident in the rigid set of his shoulders.

"Is this going to be a running theme, then?" She nodded to his empty hands. "I can start being in charge of dinner. Unless you wanted to skip eating again? Because I'm okay with that."

He didn't laugh.

"We're going out," he said shortly.

She glanced down at her yoga pants and off-the-shoulder T-shirt, which she'd changed into an hour ago. "I'm dressed for takeout."

"It doesn't matter. Avery knows we're married. And she told Bettina. The secret will probably be public knowledge by midnight. If it takes that long."

Meredith cursed. That explained his snippy mood.

The news probably wouldn't take very long to filter down to Texas, either, and then where would she be? Her father's lawyer had given her a very short time frame to settle this divorce, and he'd been clear—tell her father or he'd do it for her.

Now the press might beat him to it. She cursed again.

"Yeah." Jason's smile was grim. "That's exactly what I said."

"How did Avery find out? Oh, *no*. Not the—"

"Security camera." He nodded and pressed the spot between his brows, hard. "My best guess is we weren't as careful as we thought. Or if not that, she wasn't out of sight when I got out of the car at Hurst the other night. Somehow she saw us together and started poking her nose into my business."

"What does that mean? I can't be your spy anymore. Right?"

And if she couldn't be his spy, that meant he had to sign the divorce papers whether she got the designs or not.

Fabulous. Though she was a little sad to have no excuse to go in Avery's place to her meeting tomorrow. Despite the stolen nature of the designs, Meredith had been looking forward to seeing what happened in a fashion-house deal.

Was that why Avery had agreed to let Meredith go— because she already knew that Meredith was Jason's wife?

The back of her throat soured. So much for her stellar espionage skills. She'd looked forward to crowing over her victory with Jason tonight.

He sighed and propped a shoulder against the door frame as if his legs couldn't hold him up any longer. "It means my mother's freaking thrilled that I got married. She wants to take us to dinner tonight. I couldn't say no."

Dinner with Bettina Lynhurst? As what, a *couple*?

"Uh…it's not hard. *No.* See? Easy." Jason glared at her so hotly she shoved the door wide. "You better come in."

How had everything become so complicated?

He brushed past her as if she wasn't even standing there and flung open the closet to sift through her clothes. "Where's that gold top I brought you? Bettina likes it. You should wear it with the white cropped pants and your Stuart Weitzman sandals."

She put a palm on his arm to still his near-frantic rooting through her stuff. "As sexy as it is for a guy to expend so much effort to put clothes *on* me, chill out for a second. I don't want to go to dinner with your mom, like we're a happily married couple. There's no point in it. We're about to sign divorce papers. I'm going back to Houston."

"About that." He turned to face her and in the close

confines of the closet, the smell of his soap and his skin melded into something wholly Jason and wholly delicious.

She didn't want to notice the way he smelled, not with the calculating glint she caught in his gaze. "What about it? Don't you dare tell me I have more stuff to do before you divorce me after all. If the secret is out, my job is over. I'm not of any use to you any longer."

"Not true. I can't divorce you. Not yet."

She shook her head before he'd stopped talking. "You have to. It's over. Avery messed up your plans, and while I'm sad I don't get to tell her off, what else can I do here?"

"Bettina likes that I'm married. She actually said she can consider retiring now and would gladly turn over the reins to me since I've settled down." In a totally surprising move, he took her hand and curled her fingers around his, as if they often held hands while talking. "Avery's plan, whatever it was, backfired. Don't you see?"

It dawned on her, though how her brain still functioned with Jason's fingers brushing hers was mystifying. "You mean she did it to make you look bad. She thought Bettina would take it as an act of irresponsibility."

"Exactly. But she didn't. The opposite, in fact."

The unsettled feeling in her stomach turned into one big knot of foreboding as she connected the dots. "Let me get this straight. Your mom is all set to retire and name you as the new Lyn CEO because you got married. So you're not going to sign the divorce papers. Because it benefits you to stay married."

"In a nutshell." He dropped her hand. "I'm asking you to be my wife, out in the open. We'll make an announcement and everything, and you'll move into my condo. Once Bettina follows through with handing me the CEO job, then I'll divorce you."

"No. No way." She couldn't spit it out fast enough, especially since her heart was screaming "Yes, yes, yes" to being Jason's wife for real, for as long as it lasted. "Not for anything could you convince me this is a good idea."

It was too open-ended, too real, too rife with possibilities for her to get used to the arrangement, and then where would she be? Trying to forget Jason after a whole new level of intimacy.

He smiled and it did dangerous things to her pulse. "I'll give you whatever amount of money you were going to get as a loan from your father. Name it."

She didn't hesitate. "A hundred thousand dollars."

"Done. And now you don't have to tell your family that you messed up in Vegas. Think about it. No loan. All you have to do is fake this marriage well enough so my mother feels warm and squishy about retiring."

Crap. She'd thought he'd say no to such an outrageous sum and now she was stuck. "I can't... You want me to *live* with you? What are you saying, that we'll sleep in the same bed and stuff? Pretend we're in love?"

Her throat tightened. How long could she keep that up before it became a reality?

Forever. She'd have to keep it up forever because she was *not* falling in love with Jason. It was too dangerous.

"No to the first, yes to the second. I have a spare room."

"Of course. Sleeping with your wife is way over the line." She hadn't meant for that to come out so sarcastically.

Was she actually disappointed that he wasn't using their marriage as an excuse to play husband and wife to the fullest? Separate bedrooms actually made a sick sort of sense. It was tawdry to trade sex for a hundred thousand dollars and she'd deck him if he had suggested it.

But what if he'd suggested something totally different? Like the two of them having some kind of normal relationship full of making love and fun and togetherness. Falling asleep wrapped in each other's arms and sharing secrets in the dark. That she would have agreed to in a heartbeat because it meant he felt all the same confusing, scary things she felt.

Her mind buzzed dully with all the implications of that one crystalline realization. Maybe she wasn't so confused after all because there it was. She wanted something special and real and lasting with Jason. He didn't.

He cocked his head and contemplated her. "Sharing a bedroom complicates our interaction unnecessarily. This is a business proposition. Same as the first one."

Right, how could she forget? She wanted something he would never give her—the man buried beneath his strategy. "I know. Marriage is still your weapon of choice."

This new deal was far more difficult to agree to. She'd be insane to say no. This would solve all her problems in one, easy shot. Except for the one where she'd be acting like Jason's wife without any of the benefits, like a supportive husband who cared about her and thought she was the best thing that ever happened to him.

She'd be insane to say yes.

"I need you, Meredith." His blue eyes filled with vulnerability and her breath hitched. Not the puppy-dog eyes. She could stand anything but that. It threw her back to that time two years ago when he'd needed her. And she'd needed him.

God help her, she still did. She couldn't resist him when he morphed into that man she'd spent so many blissful hours with. It was stupid to even pretend she didn't want to stay a few more days. Stupid to pretend she'd snatched back that piece of her soul she'd given him in Vegas.

This was her chance, her very last chance, to find out if she'd made a mistake walking away from him in Vegas. And the last chance to find out if she was making a mistake wishing for something more this time.

If living in the same house couldn't afford her an opportunity to get there, nothing could. She could go back to

Houston with the knowledge that Jason wasn't the man for her and get over him, once and for all. Somehow.

"How long?" she croaked. "I do have another job, my real job, to get back to."

Which was less and less attractive the longer she stayed smack-dab in the middle of the New York fashion industry. Wedding dresses was Cara's forte, Cara's love. Meredith only worked with Cara because they were family, and her sister didn't care that Meredith brought nothing to the table other than money.

"I don't know. Maybe a couple of weeks. Is that a yes?" The hopefulness in his voice coupled with vulnerability pretty much made her choice for her.

She held up a hand before his smile grew any wider. "How can this possibly work? I don't understand what your mother thinks we've been doing for two years with no contact."

He shook his head. "She thinks we got married recently. She's all gushy over the romance of it."

"Wait a minute. So now we're going to take our marriage, pretend it's fake with each other but real to everyone else *and* lie about the timing? How does that make sense? Avery figured out we were married from somewhere and might actually know the whole story. Do you really want to give her that much leverage?"

Jason grinned instead of getting huffy about her contradicting him, like she'd expected. "I love the way your mind works. Please, my beautiful wife, tell me what we should do instead."

Rolling her eyes, she crossed her arms before she punched him. "We tell everyone we got married in Vegas and intended to get it annulled, but neither one of us could bear to go through with it. Then we reconnected because you had to get the divorce to marry Meiling. It was obvious to both of us we never stopped loving each other and you knew you could never go through with your arranged marriage and here we are."

"That's—"

"Brilliant. Duh. Always ask a woman to give you a romantic cover story."

Cover story. Because it wasn't true. There was no romance to their practical union and they weren't in love. But she couldn't stop herself from thinking about what might happen while they were living under the same roof. If she could only get him to let his guard down, like when he'd gotten so emotional about his father, she could say *Adios* to the corporate Jason Lynhurst. The man she wanted was in there and she'd entice him into making a more permanent appearance. Then, all bets were off.

His expression veered between amusement and admiration. "Great. It's all settled, then. Right?"

She sighed. "I'm the least settled I think I've ever been in my life."

"You'll be great." He waved it off as if he had the slightest clue what she was feeling, but he couldn't possibly. "And we're late for dinner. Mess up your hair and we'll act like we had a really good reason for our tardiness."

"Careful, or you'll find yourself putting your money where your mouth is."

He grinned as if she was kidding and glanced at his watch. "Gold top. White pants. Get a move on, Mrs. Lynhurst."

Mrs. Lynhurst. Why did that make her shiver with a strange combination of apprehension and wonderment? She'd come to New York for a divorce. And yet she'd agreed to tell the world she and Jason were married in hopes of turning their relationship into something more than an advantage.

She handed him the remote. "Make yourself comfortable. I plan to take a while getting ready while I practice how I'm going to tell Hurst I quit."

"But we're already late," he protested.

"You asked for a wife. You got one. And all the idio-syncrasies that come with it. Welcome to married life."

She flounced to the bathroom and the only reason she slipped into the gold top was because she never had to see Allo again. She'd throw Jason a bone for that one.

Ten

Fortunately, Bettina was still waiting patiently at the restaurant, despite the fact that Jason and Meredith walked in almost an hour past the time she'd specified. Grinning like a loon, Bettina's gaze skittered right over Jason and fastened on the woman he'd brought.

"Sorry, Mom." Jason bent to kiss her cheek and opted not to offer a lame excuse for why it had taken him nearly sixty minutes to convince his wife to let her mother-in-law buy them dinner. "This is Meredith."

"Ms. Lynhurst, it's a pleasure." Meredith held out her hand and after a perfunctory shake, she slid into the chair opposite his mother and leaned in, elbows on the table. "Your jeans are my favorite. The fit is divine. You're one of the reasons I learned to sew when I was a teenager."

Jason did a double take. That was laying it on a bit thick, wasn't it? But Meredith's face exuded sincerity and his mother was eating it up.

Bettina beamed. "Call me Bettina. I'm so happy to meet you at last. Jason is off my Christmas list for not introducing us at the Garment Center gala the other day."

"Geez, Mom."

"Oh, I know," Meredith said on top of his protest and shushed him. "I was disappointed when he hustled me out the door so soon after we'd arrived. He couldn't wait to get me alone."

With a curse, Jason took his own chair and signaled the waiter. It did not distract either woman from their conversation…which apparently didn't include him.

Bettina laughed. "I'll bet. He couldn't keep his eyes off you the entire time I was talking to him. Obviously, he was thinking about taking you home then."

"Really?" Meredith's hand found its way onto his thigh and she shot him a sideways glance that he had no trouble interpreting. It was hot and wicked and set his blood on a low simmer.

This was not exactly how he'd envisioned dinner going. Or their marriage, for that matter. This was the problem with Meredith; she had her own vision of how things should go and it rarely coincided with his.

"That's enough about the gala," Jason interjected before his mother could say something else risqué that gave Meredith the wrong idea. He wasn't hung up on Meredith like his mother had made it sound. He'd only been watching her so closely because she'd been talking to Avery.

Mostly. You couldn't blame a guy for noticing how beautiful Meredith was. Or how smart and funny and…good for his plans. *That* was her best quality, he reminded himself.

"Well, you should have told me Meredith was your wife when I mentioned her." His mother ordered an obscenely expensive bottle of wine from the waiter and waved him off to focus on Meredith again. "How do you like working for Hurst?"

Meredith wrinkled her nose. "It's got no soul. The designs are good, but not great. All the people are in it for the money, you can tell."

"I couldn't agree more." The woman *Vogue* had once dubbed the First Lady of Fashion contemplated the composed younger woman across the table. "Where did you study?"

"Meredith didn't go to college," Jason said, a little miffed that he'd been excluded from the conversation thus far.

The temperature from his wife's glare nearly gave him a sunburn and her hand slipped away from his thigh. And now that it was gone, he wished she'd put it back.

"She was talking to me." Meredith flicked a fingernail at his arm, her tone mild, but he could tell she was not happy with him. "You've had her attention for thirty-some-odd years. Now it's my turn." She refocused on Bettina. "My sister is a designer and I've been working with her for a couple of years. Other than that, I'm self-taught."

Meredith and his mother descended into a lengthy back and forth about the merits of formal education versus finding a mentor, leaving him to stew over his wine.

Why was his temper flaring? This was exactly what he'd asked for—Meredith playing up the part of his wife.

He just hadn't expected her to do it so well.

Or for his mother to like her so much. How was he going to break it to Bettina when he signed the divorce papers? He hated it when he couldn't see all the angles, hated it when he hadn't anticipated the direction a situation was going to go.

He dug into his filet mignon and asparagus tips, determined to get through this dinner so he could take Meredith back to her hotel and get her stuff. They needed to strategize on the announcement and settle her into his condo.

Letting her into his space was going to be a trick and a half. He'd never lived with a woman and had spent the past six months working through the idea of sharing his condo with Meiling. She would have respected his personal territory. She would never have barged into the bathroom with him, curling iron in one hand and a raspberry-filled donut in the other, wearing nothing but a loosely-tied robe.

When Meredith had done that, he'd ended up licking the raspberry filling from the tips of her breasts. Of course, he'd been the one to swirl it there, much to her dark-eyed delight and moans of pleasure.

Maybe she'd let him do it again.

"Isn't that right, Jason?" his mother prompted.

What had he missed during his donut-induced fantasy? "Uh… What?"

"She was telling me about the innovative partnership you spearheaded with the Style Channel." Meredith's eyebrows rose as she silently shot him get-your-crap-together vibes. "Clearly you get your fashion and business sense from your mother. And your ability to pay attention from your father."

His mother dissolved into a good, long laugh. Jason couldn't remember the last time he'd heard her laugh like that. An answering smile tugged at his mouth.

"Sweetie, we're going to get along fine," Bettina told Meredith. "And you," she said to Jason, "are back on my Christmas list for having the foresight to marry such a great woman."

Mission accomplished, he thought sourly and decided to keep his mouth shut the rest of the evening. Which he almost succeeded in doing, at least until he and Meredith slid into the car to go back to her hotel.

"Let me check you out and then I'll help you pack," he said. "You can take the weekend to get settled in."

She crossed her white-cropped-pants-clad legs and grinned. "You sure you know what you're signing up for? I am a girl. With lots of girl stuff."

"It's the least I can do." He tore his gaze from her shapely legs, but it didn't erase the sharp desire to feel them wrapped around his waist. "Thanks, by the way. For wearing the outfit I picked out and for being nice to my mother. You were great."

"You say that like your mom is a witch and I had to suffer through dinner. She's amazing. Such an inspiration. I had a hard time keeping my inner fangirl in check."

News to him. But then, they never really talked about Meredith's interests. It never occurred to him until that moment that she'd yet to share thought one about her long-term plans after buying into the wedding-dress business.

And now he was intrigued anew by this woman he'd married. "I thought you were just being nice."

She twirled a lock of mahogany hair and batted her eyes. "In that case, I expect to be well compensated for my time."

"What, a divorce and a hundred grand isn't enough for you?" he teased.

"It's a start." Her wicked smile said the compensation should also include several orgasms in a row.

Despite that, he couldn't help but ask, "Seriously, what would be enough? If you could have anything in my power to give you, what would you ask for?"

The car had almost reached her hotel, but oddly, he didn't want to end the conversation. She was a woman of deep passion and convictions and he had the strangest urge to know her better. Not because of any paranoid need to pretend their marriage was real; ten minutes into dinner with his mother, it was obvious there was no danger of anyone questioning the authenticity of it.

But because after a long day of strategy and worrying about all the angles, he just wanted to be with Meredith. Connecting. She relaxed him and he liked it. Probably too much.

"You mean besides sex?" Her gaze softened as she glanced at him. "Oh, so we're done flirting. You don't have to give me anything. This has been fun. I'm working for a top-notch designer and I'm learning a lot. Allo's horrible, but he's as much a legend as your mom. Sometimes, I feel like I was dropped into the middle of a fairy tale."

"Really?" He glanced at her, but she seemed sincere. "You never said anything about wanting to be a designer. Is that part of your dream alongside wedding dresses?"

Her brow furrowed and she hesitated.

The sign for her hotel popped into his peripheral vision and he motioned to the driver to circle the block. There was no way they were cutting this conversation short, not when he'd just realized Meredith had a hidden layer he'd yet to discover. In all their many conversations, how had this never come up? The mystery fascinated him.

"Come on," he prompted. "You know all about my stuff with my father and the split. And that was all pre-Vegas anyway, so you heard about it back then. Wedding dresses are new. Tell me what's going to happen when you get back to Houston."

They were married and he wanted to know his wife's every last secret.

Meredith curled her hands into a tight knot high in her lap and thought seriously about blowing off Jason's question with a flip comment. But she'd never talked to anyone about her plan except Cara, and her sister hadn't asked any questions. She'd hugged her and murmured something about welcoming her with open arms.

It wasn't exactly the same as a glowing endorsement of her skill set or as if she'd earned a spot because she'd busted her butt. She'd actually never even interviewed for a job in her life. How could anyone take her seriously?

Was it so wrong to want validation? To ask someone who got what she was trying to do to acknowledge her plan and say it didn't suck?

She glanced at Jason sideways. This man she'd married had design and business expertise bred into his genes. He'd grown up immersed in the world of couture. And he'd seen her naked. Who better to bare her soul to? She'd done the same in Vegas and it had been a part of their connection.

"I'll become a partner in a successful business," she stated firmly. "Like a real grown-up."

"What are you now?" Jason's blue eyes glinted with amusement. "A fake one?"

Yeah, so that was why she should have kept her mouth shut. For a moment, she'd forgotten all the soul-baring in

Vegas had centered on their mutual lack of direction. He'd found his and apparently thought it was funny that she hadn't.

She glared at him. "I'm not anything right now. Former beauty queen. Allo's lackey. Wife to Jason Lynhurst. Soon-to-be wedding-dress-business owner. That's the extent of my identity."

He sobered and took her hand to kiss the knuckles. "That's a pretty good list of things to be proud of. How many other wives do I have? You're one of a kind."

She rolled her eyes. *Men.* Or maybe it was just Jason who was that full of himself. "So, I'm supposed to think it's some honor that we're still married? Marriage is one of the many weapons in your arsenal, right?"

"Yeah, and I don't wield my rocket launcher indiscriminately," he pointed out quietly. "If you weren't valuable to me, I'd have signed the papers on day one and found another strategic marriage. Why do you think I've fought so hard to keep you?"

That set her back. How had he managed to make that sound so romantic? Her stomach fluttered and she rubbed the spot as she flailed for something to say.

"Because I rock your socks, obviously. That's the only reason I can think of," she mumbled.

"Don't sell yourself short, Meredith." He stroked her hand until she glanced at him. "You'd be an amazing asset to anyone. Your sister is lucky to have you as a partner, especially if you're as good at designing wedding dresses as you are at understanding the business angles."

"Now you're just humoring me." She smiled to dispel the contradiction. "And I'm probably equally good at both, which is not very. Honestly, I don't know the first thing about designing wedding dresses. I can sew and cut patterns, which is why Cara keeps me around."

The thought sent a frisson of fear up her spine. Actually, she hadn't gotten as far in the plan as to what would happen once she returned to Houston and handed over money to her sister. She'd kind of thought that would be it and then she'd magically feel like an adult.

But what would happen the next day? Would Cara expect Meredith to start doing *her* job and design something? Was that part of the partnership deal?

Seemed like a phone call to her sister was in order, pronto. All this needed to be ironed out or she would fail.

"You can learn design if that's your goal," Jason said mildly. "Or you can work the business side. Make it what you want."

"You say that like I have all this flexibility." In reality, she was doing the one thing available to her. It wasn't like she could start her *own* business.

Or could she?

Her brain turned that over from all angles. If Jason gave her the money and she didn't have a loan, the possibilities were endless. When she'd left Houston, Cara Chandler-Harris Designs had been the be-all and end-all. But Jason had expanded her worldview enormously. Maybe wedding dresses wasn't the only thing she could do. Or the only thing that would work to get her where she wanted to be.

"Don't you have flexibility? This is your dream, sweetheart." He tipped her chin up and sucked her into his gaze, holding her attention like a hypnotist. "Don't spend your life doing something that doesn't speak to you. Lynhurst Enterprises is my heritage, built from the ground up by people who gave me life and share my blood. I'd do anything, sacrifice everything, to keep it afloat. What are you that passionate about?"

The fire in his expression and conviction in his voice mesmerized her. She loved it when he forgot to be the mastermind and spilled what was in his soul.

"I...don't know." But she wanted to name something in the worst way, especially if it kept them in this place of connection. Random thoughts, snippets of ideas formed on her tongue. "I love clothes, love the feel of fabrics, the art of fit and color. I've dabbled in design, but I think I'm better at seeing what doesn't work than at creating something from scratch."

"Good. What else? Talk to me more about your impressions of Hurst, like you did with Bettina."

"Hurst is *interesting*." The most politically correct word she could use to describe an environment slightly less welcoming than a room full of Miss Texas contenders when they realized you were a Chandler. "But Lyn is something else. Like Disney World for lovers of fashion. I know I was only there for a few minutes, but as soon as I walked through the doors, it hit me here."

She touched the center of her chest with a finger, but his intent gaze didn't leave her face.

"Why?" he prompted.

"Because the ambience was, I don't know, alive." Bit by bit, his attentiveness and genuine interest spurred her to articulate things she'd hardly recognized prior to this. "Like the creative spirit had soaked into the walls. I had the strangest physical reaction. Giddiness. Expectation. You probably think I'm crazy."

"No, I think you're speaking like a woman who has couture in her soul. Keep it up and I might throw in an executive job at Lyn along with the 100K," he advised with a brow lift.

With a sharp inhale, she searched his expression. "An executive job? At Lyn? Where in the world did that come from? We were talking about me owning half a wedding-dress business. I'm not executive material."

He shrugged. "I say differently, and I'm pretty sure I qualify as an expert at what it takes since I've hired a few executives in my life. Is it really that much of a surprise that I think you're incredible? You naturally think strategically and you honor your commitments. You show up and work hard. Those are all qualities of successful executives. Your love of fashion is a bonus."

"I can't work at Lyn," she protested and bit her lip as the image of an office with *Meredith Chandler-Harris* on the door materialized in her mind. And wouldn't dissolve. "I have a job. With my sister. Besides, I live in Houston."

But in New York, no one knew her. If she made it here, she could say indisputably that she'd done it on her own—without Cara, without her father's money and influence, without her mother's social connections, without the title of Former Miss Texas.

She'd never thought that would feel so necessary and important until this conversation with Jason.

"People move for jobs all the time."

Never in a million years would she have thought she might be in a position to accept…because she'd elected to stay in New York. If she did, she'd see Jason every day. *Every day.*

That thought gave her a physical reaction that far eclipsed the one she'd experienced when walking into Lyn. Hope and anticipation uncurled in her chest. And then she had to squash it before it rooted too deeply. "More importantly, we're about to get divorced."

"What's that got to do with anything? Divorced people can work together, if they're both mature about it."

"Your parents couldn't," she pointed out before she thought about how it would come across.

His gaze darkened. "Yeah, but they were in love once. We won't have that problem."

"Right." That somehow didn't make it any better. Because all at once, she wanted Jason to be as passionate about her as he was about Lyn.

Once, he had been. And the taste of it had stuck with her for two years.

She was still in New York due to that as much as or more than the opportunity to work at a genuine fashion house, if she was being honest. The divorce wasn't even a factor. Maybe it hadn't been for quite some time.

"Think about it. It was a sincere offer." He glanced away as the car rolled to a stop at the curbside of her hotel. "Let's get your stuff. It's been a long day already."

Meredith took his hand to allow him to help her from the car, her mind in a whirl of confused emotions and trepidation and a strange sense of determination. Because she got it now. At the same time she pulled passion out of Jason, he pulled it out of her. It just revealed itself in different ways.

She wouldn't be executive material in Houston. She probably wouldn't even be a good wedding-dress-business partner. And she definitely wouldn't make that leap from Former Miss Texas to Full-Fledged Adult because only with Jason's guiding influence and help and support could she truly succeed. She needed him, needed his belief in her, needed him to goad her into stretching and growing her skill set.

Most of all, she needed him because, despite her confusion and protests to the contrary, she was pretty sure she was falling in love with this man she'd accidentally married, who'd slowly let her peel back his layers, exactly as she'd hoped. Who also wanted to use their marriage to get himself into the CEO's office and then divorce her.

What was she going to do?

Eleven

Jason's loft condo on 12th Avenue was the most gorgeous piece of real estate Meredith had ever seen. And that was including the mayor of Houston's house, her parents' house and Lyn Couture's office.

"Oh, my God, Jason," she breathed when she walked through the door to take in the floor-to-ceiling glass on three sides that displayed the illuminated New York skyline like a photograph.

But it wasn't a still life; the vibrant city zipped by in a string of lights, people and vehicles. To the west, the Hudson flowed to the Atlantic, while high above, she and Jason watched from the hushed, darkened atmosphere of his home.

Ebony hardwood floors polished to a high sheen reflected the city's movements, and when Jason snapped on the lights, she gasped again as the open floor plan spread out around her. The stainless-steel and grey granite kitchen looked like something out of a magazine, and the masculine furnishings accented the huge living area creatively to block out individual rooms despite the lack of walls.

An angular staircase zigzagged from the hardwood to the second floor, where she could see another sitting area beyond the glass divider, as well as two doors leading to what were probably the bedrooms.

And this was where she would stay for however long she could finagle it. With Jason. It made her a little faint.

Dropping her shoulder bag, she put a hand on his arm and leaned in with as grave an expression as she could muster. "I mean this in all seriousness. Can I have the condo in the divorce?"

"Not unless you have a really good lawyer," he deadpanned with a wry twist of his lips. "I take it that means you like it."

"It's breathtaking. I had no idea something like this existed. I mean, you see the pictures in magazines and you think they used Photoshop or something to make the views so spectacular."

With a grin, he picked up the bag she'd dropped and hefted the other one, then nodded for her to precede him toward the stairs. "It's smaller than some places and not in a trendy neighborhood. But I like it."

She could tell. The furnishings and decor had Jason Lynhurst stamped all over them. This place was clearly something he took pride in, and inside these walls, she'd bet he forgot all about his suits and business deals. She was dying to find out.

He bid her good-night at the door of her room and she let him go with no small amount of regret. It was appropriate to sleep apart. Sleeping in the same bed had implications. Hell if she could remember what they were right this minute, but she'd make the best of it.

Well, this was no different than sleeping alone in a hotel room. But that was before she'd realized how strong her feelings for Jason were becoming.

Her room was small but functional, with a tiny window that let in almost no moonlight, but the room was along the interior of the building. At least the bedroom had an en suite bathroom so she didn't have to parade through the upstairs sitting area to get to the other one.

She turned on all the lights and got ready for bed, but sleep didn't come easily. Jason's surprise job offer churned through her mind. Being Cara's assistant was more her speed, but it was safe and familiar. Was that what she wanted? What was New York if it wasn't a place to take a leap?

Of course, Jason could very well recant in the cold light of morning. After all, he had a history of making rash decisions and then taking them back the next day.

At some point, she fell asleep. A vivid dream took her down a rabbit hole of confusion. Jason was gone. She had a sense of being alone…and frightened…

She awoke in a cold sweat, startled and with no clue where she was. All at once, reality settled over her. She was in New York, in Jason's loft.

Chest heaving, she tried to calm her racing heart. Nothing she did worked. Her heart beat erratically and painfully in her chest and she couldn't catch her breath.

Whose stupid idea was it to sleep in separate bedrooms? Meredith was flesh and blood and wanted Jason's comforting arms around her. Right now.

Slipping from the bed, she padded out of her room and across the sitting area before her screaming conscience could remind her that they'd agreed it was better not to sleep together.

Jason's door was ajar. She let herself in, pausing for a moment to let her eyes adjust. The bed took shape and then she just barely made out the sleeping form in it.

Jason. Her heart sighed in relief.

She slipped beneath the sheet and rolled into his warm body. Pulse settling, she breathed in his scent, and it triggered something incredibly relaxing. It came back to her on a flash of memory—sleeping with him like this in Vegas. Sheer bliss. She loved curling up against his back.

But then he sighed and flipped over, disrupting her position.

"Uh, sleeping here," he muttered and said something else unintelligible.

"I had a bad dream," she whispered. Out of nowhere, her voice broke on a sob.

"Hey," he said softly and his fingers slid through her hair, his thumb featherlight against her jaw. "God, Meredith. You're shaking."

He shifted, reaching behind him to what had to be a bedside table. With a snick and a whir, a dark curtain behind the bed rose, spilling light over them. The whole wall behind the head of the bed was glass, and the skyline he'd revealed was almost as gorgeous as her husband. Jason lay spread out in his bed, sheet at his waist and one hand under the pillow as he faced her.

Not so much of a cure for her racing heart, then.

He tilted her chin to look her in the eye, evaluating. "Come here," he instructed and lifted an arm in invitation. "You're freezing."

Yes, she was. On the inside, where she couldn't reach it. Ice ran through her veins, overwhelming her all at once.

Unable to stop shaking, she nestled her backside into his torso and when the heavy weight of his arm dropped against her waist, she closed her eyes, fully at peace for the first time in…forever.

Lacing her fingers through his, she absorbed his body heat and let it soak into her bones, liquefying them. "This wasn't a cheap ploy to get into your bed. I swear. This isn't about sex."

He was silent for a moment, nestling her a little tighter against him. "I could see for myself that it wasn't. Better now?"

"Yeah. Thanks."

His thumb absently stroked hers. She wondered if he even realized how comforting it was. How greatly she'd needed him. But he couldn't possibly know because she hadn't told him. Regardless, he'd instinctively guessed the exact right thing to do to make her feel better.

And this was not like Vegas at all. It was far, far better than she could have ever imagined.

"What was your dream about?" he asked softly.

Bits and pieces of it floated back to her. "I was looking for...something."

It had been on the tip of her tongue to spill all the images and emotions from her dream. How she'd dashed out to the street in her lacy pajama top and shorts, searching for any sign of Jason's familiar form. How she couldn't find him.

But she didn't say any of that. Interpreting the dream wasn't difficult. She was scared of losing him and had no idea how to hold on to him.

"Something important?" Jason prompted.

"Critically. But I couldn't find it and it scared me." She sighed. "Sounds stupid to be so scared over that."

Especially since her real fear was the exact opposite— that she'd continue to have daily contact with Jason for the foreseeable future and it would be torturous because it wouldn't unfold like she'd desperately come to want. She wished for their relationship to be like *this*. Holding each other in the dark. Whispering about their dreams and failures and uncertainties. Being there for each other. Loving each other.

And that wasn't the marriage she'd signed up for. She couldn't even open her mouth and tell him her secrets.

"Fear isn't something we can rationalize." His voice drifted and she realized he was tired but fighting to stay awake. For her sake.

"Sorry I woke you up. I just needed to feel safe. Don't kick me out."

"'Kay."

His arm grew heavier and his breathing even. And he didn't so much as roll away from her even a little. He cared about her; there was no mistaking it. It just wasn't enough.

Maybe it was time to figure out what could be enough.

Jason woke all at once, extremely aware of two things: one, the raised curtain let in a hell of a lot of sunlight for 6:00 a.m. Two, Meredith was in his bed, snugged up against him, spoon-style, despite an ocean of bed on the other side of her.

And he liked her exactly where she was. His lower half firmly approved and raised the flag in joyful salute.

That was bad. She'd come to him in the middle of the night looking for a security blanket, not a lover. He couldn't take advantage of her. They'd agreed to a civil relationship conducted in separate bedrooms. Like what he would have had with Meiling.

She made a noise in her throat and arched, presumably in a just-waking-up stretch. Her bottom grazed his groin and her noise transformed into a sexy moan. She murmured his name and snuggled closer.

He groaned. Who was he kidding? He hadn't married Meiling. He'd married Meredith and he couldn't resist her. Not now, not ever. She was in his bed, in his head, drugging him with her seductive lure. Fisting his hands in the fabric at her hips, he hauled her closer, as she twisted against his erection in a slow, sensuous, deliberate slide.

Need exploded in his midsection, urging him to slake his thirst in his wife's sweet center.

"Meredith," he growled. She had four seconds to vacate his bed or reap the consequences. Which would be a very delicious and well-deserved punishment indeed.

"Yeah, hon?"

"*Now* it's about sex."

"You better believe it."

That was all the encouragement he needed. His boxer shorts hit the floor.

In seconds, he peeled the lacy top and shorts off her killer body and threw them over his shoulder, then spooned her back into place. He nipped at her throat at the same moment she reached back to guide his hands to her breasts. Hot and firm, they filled his palms, and he explored her peaked nipples at his leisure until she pushed deeper into his hands, silently begging for more.

"I need you now," she murmured thickly and her desire zinged through him.

He had a goddess in his bed, in his arms, and he wanted to be inside her, pleasuring her, completing her, while she filled him from the inside out with her unique power.

Groaning with the effort, he rolled away and fumbled in his nightstand for the condoms that he was pretty sure were still there from his last relationship…which had ended six or eight months ago if he recalled. His fingers closed around one and miraculously, he got it into place without losing it altogether.

He slid into heaven a moment later. She gasped and tilted her hips, drawing him deeper. The perfection sent him into an upward spiral, nearly initiating a premature explosion he wasn't ready for.

"Wait," he gasped and stilled her writhing body with a flat hand to her stomach.

"Uh, no." She thrust backward, and his eyes crossed as the pressure built. "You feel amazing. I can't wait. Touch me."

With no clue how he'd held back, he complied, fingering her center with quick, firm circles and letting her set the frantic pace until she stiffened and cried out. Ripples of her fierce climax set off his and he buried himself to the hilt with a hoarse cry.

Spent, he held her close, reveling in the heat and sensation bleeding through his body.

"You feel free to have a nightmare any night you choose," he muttered into her hair.

She didn't respond for so long, he wondered if maybe she hadn't heard him. Or maybe he'd said the wrong thing. "You okay?"

She rolled to face him and he missed the feel of her body against his.

"What are we doing here?"

Connecting. Exactly like he'd imagined, except better. She belonged in his bed. "I was taking advantage of the fact that it's Saturday. What were you doing?"

Her brows drew together. "I mean with us. I didn't climb into your bed with the intent of seducing you."

He hid a smile. "Is that what you did? Oh, no. I feel all compromised and stuff."

"Stop making jokes and listen. This is serious. We're married. We're living in the same house. We slept together last night and you held me through the remnants of a nightmare. Then we woke up to indulge in wicked, hot morning sex. All things real couples do. What part of this marriage is fake?"

All vestiges of good humor fled as her meaning sank in. "I guess… Well, when you put it that way, none of it is."

"Yeah. This is as real as it gets. And I don't think I can do it any other way."

"You mean you want to share a bedroom and be a couple?" How he got that out with a straight face was beyond him. Because that cart was already a mile down the road ahead of the horse. All they were doing now was chasing it down so the cart and horse could have a conversation about how they'd be hooked together.

Her gaze fastened on to his and wouldn't let him shake loose. "Is that what you want?"

He waited to feel a sense of panic or dread, but nothing materialized. Why not have a 100-percent real marriage, at least until they signed the papers? The benefits suited him pretty well and the more lovey-dovey they came across to his mother, the better.

He could sleep with Meredith every night. The thought made him downright light-headed with glee.

"It's not what I thought would happen," he said slowly. This was the core of his problem with Meredith; she messed up his vision. Instead of balking against it, maybe it was time to embrace it. "But I'm not opposed to it. If you're not."

As long as they both understood this was still a marriage with a purpose, all would be well. Under no circumstances could he allow any sort of emotion to be tied to this marriage. That's when all the problems happened. The second he gave her any leverage over him—or worse, fell for her—she'd mess him up. Jason refused to be the kind of leader who let emotional distractions ruin a company. One Lynhurst with that track record was enough.

"I'm not." Her smile grew tremulous. "It just scares me."

"What, the idea of having a non-fake marriage?" He shrugged. "It's not so different than what we've been doing."

That was the key. Everything should—and could—stay the same.

She sat up, clutching the sheet to her chest, but not very well, and one nipple peeked out over the top. She couldn't have struck a more erotic pose if a men's magazine photographer had positioned her. Somehow, he didn't think she'd appreciate knowing she'd turned him on all over again in the middle of her serious discussion.

"Jason, we've never dated. Never had that getting-to-know-you period. It's not like we can go backward. This is all too real, too fast. It doesn't terrify you?"

"The only thing that scares me is the thought of doing anything that jeopardizes my merger plans. As long as you're not in the way of that, what's the problem? We live together for a few weeks, get my mother comfortable with retiring and file the divorce papers. I'll take you out on as many dates as you want."

She stared at him as if he'd lost all of his marbles and then tried to take some of hers. "Why would we still get a divorce?"

All the air left the room. "Wait, when did we start talking about not getting a divorce?"

He couldn't be married to Meredith long-term, letting her influence him and coerce him into losing his brain on a regular basis. The promise of divorce gave him a time box. He couldn't lose that out.

"That's the crux of this whole conversation." She shook her head. "Neither one of us *needs* a divorce any longer. This is a matter of what we want now. You weren't going to divorce Meiling after a few weeks, were you? Why is our relationship different?"

"Because it is," he sputtered, scrambling to figure out why this part of the conversation *did* scare him. "Her culture frowns on divorce, and the textile agreements would have been long-term anyway."

The atmosphere turned frigid as she watched him.

The fear uncoiling in his belly actually felt an awful lot like denial. He couldn't have married Meiling. He was *glad* he hadn't married Meiling. It probably would have been exactly the marriage he envisioned and he'd be unaware the entire time how unhappy he was.

But what would make him happy? Meredith? How could he possibly know that before making a mistake that couldn't be easily undone? Or worse, before letting her into his heart where she might become more important than Lynhurst Enterprises?

This was backward and inside out. He *should* be telling her whatever she wanted to hear so he could keep her in place by his side. He needed to stay married. What Meredith suggested suited his plans to a T.

Why wasn't he saying yes and worrying about the fallout later? "You and Meiling are different. Leave it at that."

"So you're okay with landing your CEO job under false pretenses and then telling your mom you're getting a divorce within a few days? She's giving you that job in good faith." Her gaze tried and convicted him. "Is that really the kind of man you want me to believe you are?"

No. He wanted to scream it. But he couldn't speak,

couldn't think around the roaring in his head. The question was too big to answer and too big to not answer.

She didn't wait for him to figure it out.

"So as long as I'm convenient, I'm allowed to stick around and sleep in your bed. I get it." Her mouth firmed into a flat line that conveyed exactly how disappointing she found this whole conversation. "This is still about how your marriage affects your merger plans. If I outlive my usefulness, then I get the ax. Even after last night...and this morning."

Last night, when he'd held her close and breathed in her scent and it was every bit as wonderful as he'd remembered.

Something hitched in his chest as he saw very clearly what she'd hoped they were discussing. That their marriage could become real in every sense. Emotionally *and* physically. Her feelings were all over her face and glinting from her gaze. It sucked at him, encouraging him to spill things from his own heart. Things that shouldn't be there because they led to bad decisions.

The pain behind his rib cage intensified. He had to shut down her hopes for anything more than the business arrangement they'd agreed to. "What else would you expect our marriage to be about?"

A shutter dropped over her expression and she looked away. "Nothing. Sounds great. Glad we talked. Let me know when you decide what's happening with our marriage. I'm going to take a shower."

Wordlessly, he watched her flee the bed. He knew he'd upset her, but he lacked the ability to fix it. And it hurt. He didn't like disappointing her and he didn't like not knowing what she might do about it. Would she leave him? That thought scared him more than the idea of staying married forever.

Yep. This was definitely a real marriage now, for better or worse.

* * *

Meredith didn't bring up the subject of marriage again. Neither did she speak to him in more than monosyllables for the remainder of the weekend. She didn't even say good-bye when he left for the office Monday morning.

Three days into this marriage that never should have happened and it was already a disaster. Twice during the course of the morning, he reached for the phone to call her and broach the subject of their divorce and stopped.

What would he say? He definitely didn't want a divorce. But he wasn't prepared to articulate why, even to himself. Though his brain had no problem reminding him constantly that if they got divorced, she might find someone else, and he couldn't stomach the image of another man's hands on Meredith.

On the flip side, he was equally unprepared to hear all of Meredith's terms for a real marriage. How was he supposed to have a normal relationship? Lynhurst DNA laced his chromosomes, which apparently rendered males senseless when they got around a woman who was hot for them.

But he and Meredith couldn't stay in limbo forever. They'd have to talk about it eventually.

It took the company grapevine about thirty minutes to send the news around that Jason Lynhurst had gotten married and his new wife had been working for Hurst. People dropped by all day to congratulate him, which he accepted with sincere thanks.

They didn't have to know there might be a divorce on the horizon. Or there might not be.

The one person he didn't talk to was Meredith.

He kept expecting her name to pop up on his phone, maybe with a sexy text message or a suggestion that he come home for lunch. Not that he'd been fantasizing about that or anything.

He watched the clock until after one and cursed when he realized he'd been hoping she'd at least take two minutes to let him know she was okay. Or what she'd done all day to keep herself occupied while he was at work.

She didn't. He tried not to think about her during the interminably long day, but failed. Miserably. Her feelings were probably still hurt, and being responsible for that dug at him worse than not talking to her.

At five after five, he couldn't stand the silence and he couldn't stand any more brooding about it. This was ridiculous. At the very least, he and Meredith were going to be married for a few more weeks. They couldn't go on like this.

He went straight home, irritation just this side of boiling over, and it made him even angrier that he had no good reason to be mad. When he stormed into the loft, she was standing in the foyer, filling his house with her presence, and it hit him in the gut. His temper drained away.

"Hey," he croaked and cleared his throat.

She was so lush and beautiful and he loved that he could come home to her. She lived with him because she'd chosen to. Why that mattered, he had no clue. But it did.

"Hey," she returned coolly, her smile strained. "I was going out. Hope you don't mind."

Enough was enough. He slammed the door with one hand and with the other, he yanked her into his embrace and growled, "I do mind."

Then he poured all his frustration and longing into a scorching kiss. He hadn't planned it, but he couldn't go one more second without her in his arms. She was his wife and right now, he wanted her to know it.

She softened under his mouth and her hands clutched his shoulders weakly as he backed her against the door.

God, he'd missed her. They'd only been apart a few hours, but that was long enough for him to go numb. The taste of her zinged along his nerve endings, waking him up. And he wanted more, wanted her raw and open to him.

Wanted to take her, right here, right now, so there was no question that she belonged to him.

Clearly of the same mind, she moaned, and one leg slid along his sensuously, electrifying his senses. Their tongues melded as he yanked her silk blouse from the waistband of her skirt and snaked a hand inside, running a palm down the globe of her gorgeous rear end.

She wiggled out of her panties in a flash. His eyelids flew shut as he dipped a finger in her accessible, wet center. *Perfection.* The feel of her slick readiness went straight to his head, sensitizing him, and he craved possession. Fully. Irreversibly. Before he knew it, she'd unzipped his pants, releasing him into her eager fingers. Stroking him with a throaty moan, she lifted a leg and hooked it behind his waist, grinding her damp sex against his bare flesh.

"Now. Make me come," she commanded.

As if he could wait.

He slid into her with a groan and they joined. A flash of heat and something wholly amazing encompassed him as he made love to his wife against the door of their home. No condom, no pretending, nothing other than two people who completed each other.

His chest hurt as something inside him swelled.

He couldn't possibly possess her because it was the other way around. She owned him. Wholly. And had for some time. That's what he'd been trying to avoid, but it was too late to pretend he didn't feel anything for Meredith.

She shuddered and climaxed in three hard thrusts, finishing him off, as well.

They slumped together, and he was physically unable to separate from her. "I'm not going to apologize. I had to have you. I couldn't wait."

Sated and glowing, she glanced up at him through her lashes and smiled. "I wasn't confused. You've made quite a habit out of seducing me."

"Me? *You're* the one who comes on to me every waking

moment." He grinned back because he didn't hate it. It was a huge turn-on to be the object of her lust.

She blinked. "You realize that every time we've had sex, you've initiated it. Right?"

No, he hadn't. *She* was the sex goddess, enticing him to sample her gorgeous wares like a mythical Athena. "You're…"

And then he thought back. In the car. On the desk. Saturday morning, in bed. This afternoon, against the door. It was the sexual equivalent of the board game Clue and all the cards pointed to Jason.

"Not complaining," she finished for him. "But since you can't keep your hands off me, I'll start carrying condoms on my person at all times. The last thing we need is an accidental pregnancy to make our divorce complete."

Yes, that would put the icing on his upside-down cake of a life.

"Let me take you to dinner. No more divorce talk," he murmured. "Not now."

Not while he was still sorting through what in the hell Meredith had done to his careful plans to stay completely disentangled from his wife.

Twelve

Dinner was less strained than Meredith had expected. Of course she'd been thoroughly mellowed by the hot and quick orgasm courtesy of Lyn's chief operating officer.

He'd taken her against the door and then taken her to an outrageously expensive restaurant, flirting with her over lobster and crisp sauvignon blanc. Then he'd held her hand in the car and chatted all the way home about various topics like what he should give his mom for her birthday next week and whether Meredith would like to update the decor in his loft. Because he wanted her to feel at home.

She took it all in with a dollop of suspicion. Just a few days ago, he'd hemmed and hawed about the kind of marriage he really wanted: short-term vs. long-term, real vs. fake, same bed vs. separate beds. It was madness and she was thoroughly sick of being confused and scared that he'd never let himself be the caring, sensitive man she only got to experience when he forgot about being the mastermind, usually in the dark. That man would have no problem believing they could have a relationship based on something other than what was advantageous for Lyn.

That Jason was the one she loved and the one she wanted. She hadn't given up hope that he'd eventually be that man permanently. *That* Jason might actually admit it if he developed feelings for her in return.

Was she crazy to hang around waiting for that miracle to happen?

At quarter till nine, Jason's cell phone rang as they were walking through the door of his loft after dinner. He glanced at it and mouthed, "Avery," and answered. After a couple of "Uh-huhs" and a "We'll be here," he hung up and raised an eyebrow. "She wants to talk to us. Both of us."

Foreboding flooded Meredith's chest. "About what?"

"She didn't say. But she mentioned it was important. Do you mind?"

Avery with a secret mission sounded like the opposite of fun. Meredith sighed. She'd been fantasizing about taking a long, hot bath in Jason's enormous garden tub that overlooked the skyline. "It's fine. I'll open a bottle of wine. Unless you think it's not a social visit?"

He shrugged. "Avery is about as social as a black widow. Open the wine for us. So we can tolerate her."

Somehow that got a smile out of her. She selected a Merlot from Jason's well-stocked wine rack and pulled the cork. The pop coincided with the doorbell. Avery must have been in the lobby when she called.

Jason answered the door while Meredith poured three big glasses. Then added another quarter inch of wine to hers. For fortification. Either this surprise visit would be her second "real marriage" test at the hands of Jason's family or Avery planned to litter the loft with the shrapnel of whatever new bomb she had in store in her campaign to become CEO of Lynhurst Enterprises.

What else could she possibly be here for?

Avery swept into the room, not one blond hair out of place. Her chic Hurst House suit outclassed all of the women's outfits in a five-block radius, as always, because Avery wore clothes like everyone else wore skin—effortlessly and as if everything she put on had been created specifically for her. Meredith had never seen the woman miss a trick when it came to dressing for the occasion.

It was a talent Meredith envied despite her personal feelings for Jason's sister.

"Avery," Meredith greeted smoothly. "How nice of you to drop by. That suit is divine. Wine?"

Jason glanced at her sideways, but she ignored him. Southern manners had been bred into her since she was old enough to tell the difference between a teaspoon and a soupspoon, and sibling rivalry couldn't pry graciousness from her. At least not right out of the gate. When Avery got to the point of this visit, all bets were off.

"Thank you." Avery nodded and took the long-stemmed glass from Meredith's hand. "Sorry for the short notice. I'm glad you were free."

"Of course," she allowed. If nothing else, Avery had piqued their curiosity. Deliberately, she was sure.

Meredith indicated the sofa facing the Hudson in an invitation to Avery to take a seat, and then sank onto the other sofa next to Jason and handed him his glass of wine. Wasn't this cozy?

She gulped a third of her wine in thirty seconds as Jason put an arm around her. It was a clear message to both her and Avery. Meredith and Jason were a team, regardless of the blood flowing through the Lynhurst veins.

The show of solidarity touched her and she had to school her expression before she melted into a mushy puddle. His thumb stroked her waist and she managed to shoot him a small smile that conveyed none of her surprise at how normal it felt to sit with him in the home they shared, entertaining.

Avery's gaze cut between the two of them. "I have to confess, part of me wanted to see for myself that you were really a couple."

"You mean you didn't already know that we've been married for two years?" Jason asked in a flat tone that said if she denied it, he'd call her a liar.

"I knew," she conceded readily. "I thought it was a much more scandalous story than it apparently is."

More scandalous than a drunken, accidental Vegas

wedding that shouldn't have happened? What in the world would have qualified for *that* honor?

"Sorry to disappoint you," Jason shot back with a glower. "If you only came here to check up on me, you can leave."

Meredith put a calming hand on his arm, a little amused that playing the composed half of their couple had fallen to her. "It's okay, honey. It's natural for people to be curious, especially your family."

With an evaluating once-over, Avery zeroed in on her. "That's not the only reason I'm here. I actually came to congratulate you on your marriage. And on getting one up on me. I wasn't going to use the stolen designs, or at least not the way I led you to believe. I was dead sure I had a Lyn spy at Hurst and I planted them in hopes of flushing out the culprit."

I knew it! The after-hours project wasn't real.

"Guess it worked," Meredith responded mildly, but it took every ounce of Miss Texas in her blood to keep the shock off her face.

It had been a trap. The whole time. Normally Meredith prided herself on reading people, especially women, but this was something else. If she wasn't so furious, she might be impressed.

Avery's smile chilled the air. "I left Meredith alone that night on purpose, hoping to catch her. Imagine my surprise when I reviewed the security tapes and saw my brother in cahoots with the spy."

"Called it," Jason murmured. "So you felt compelled to figure out our association. Nice."

"For all the good it did. Mom flipped and not the way I intended." Avery made a big show of sipping her wine and then commented, "You certainly managed to come out of this the winner, didn't you?"

Clutching his chest in a mock heart attack, Jason smirked. "Hurt much to admit that?"

"Not as much as what I'm about to admit." With a Gallic

shrug, Avery focused on Meredith again. "When you called me this morning to resign, I wasn't surprised. I wouldn't have welcomed you back. Until Allo stormed into my office and threatened to quit unless I hired you back. Apparently HR quite gleefully informed him it was my fault you left."

"What?" The wineglass tilted in Meredith's suddenly numb hand and only Jason's quick reflexes kept it off the pristine white throw rug. "Allo hates me."

"Allo hates everyone," Jason and Avery both said at the same time.

"Be that as it may," Avery continued with a wry twist of her lips, "he was quite adamant that you are the best assistant he's ever had and will not cross the threshold of Hurst again until you agree to come back."

Meredith was already shaking her head. "Not interested."

She had job offers coming out of the woodwork: a yet-to-be-defined executive's job from Jason and now this. And half a wedding-dress business that she could still buy into if New York dropped off the face of the map. Or she could take the money Jason was paying her to hold off on the divorce and live in Timbuktu as a basket weaver.

"I don't think you understand," Avery broke into the swirl of Meredith's thoughts impatiently. "I cannot lose Allo. He is Hurst's premier designer and without him, we'd fold in six months. I'd pay you two-fifty in a heartbeat if that's what it took."

Confused, Meredith stared at her. "Two-fifty what? Dollars?"

"Two hundred-and-fifty *thousand*. A year. I'd pay you a quarter of a million dollars annually to ensure my company doesn't go under."

Oh, my God. The sum made her vision black out for a moment.

The number of choices suddenly open to her pounded through her head. She had choices…and *Avery's offer didn't require her to stay married to Jason.* There was absolutely nothing holding her to him any longer. If she accepted, she didn't need Jason's money. New York was wide-open to her.

She had no reason to stay in this marriage other than the obvious one—she'd still be married to Jason.

"Allo's a pain in the ass. He treated Meredith like dirt, and even if he apologized on his hands and knees, she's too good to waste her talent on him," Jason countered fiercely. "But I'll shut up now because it's her decision."

Okay, *that* was the most romantic thing he'd ever said. The warmth of his hand against her waist bled through her, arrowing straight to her heart and swelling it tenderly.

Did he realize that she alone held the power to end this rivalry between Jason and Avery by simply declining Avery's offer?

Avery would be publicly humiliated, Hurst would be in trouble and Jason could save the day with his merger plans. No one would ever consider making Avery CEO of the newly merged company, not when she had driven off the jewel in Hurst's crown.

But if Meredith did that, she'd be feeding the mastermind, not nurturing the man she loved.

It was all too much.

Shooting to her feet, she set down her empty wineglass. "I appreciate the offer, but it's been a long day. I'll have to let you know."

Avery stood, as well, obviously recognizing that she was being dismissed. "I won't take no for an answer. I can make your life very difficult if you refuse. You know where to find me."

It must be killing her that Meredith's hand held all the aces. And that was the only reason she didn't bust Avery in the mouth and spill blood all over that gorgeous suit. "I do know where to find you. Which means you might want to reconsider threatening me."

Despite her show of bravado, Meredith's hands started

to shake. Houston sounded mighty nice, and all at once, she longed to escape the politics and threats and manipulation.

Jason escorted his sister out and immediately came back to engulf Meredith in his embrace, murmuring reassuring phrases into her hair. Burying her head in his shoulder, she let his touch wash through her, calming her, warming her. And now *he* was the composed one. Apparently they were going to tag-team.

She sniffed and choked off a flood of emotionally laden words that she wouldn't be able to take back.

"You okay?" he said softly and pulled back to caress her cheek. "I'm sorry she upset you. Avery doesn't pull punches."

Normally, Meredith didn't pull punches, either, but Jason had her all messed up and emotional over every little thing. "That's the reason I'm still here. You can't take her on by yourself."

His smile settled her in a way she'd never have expected. "Maybe not, but I can take *you* on by myself."

With that, he swept her into his arms and carried her upstairs to his bed, where he undressed her so carefully and reverently, she couldn't speak. Once she was naked, he palmed the remote and clicked open the curtain. It whirred up to let in the neon night and he stared at her, worshipping her with his gaze.

"Jason, I—"

"Want me to make love to you? That was the plan."

And then he did exactly that, silently ministering to her pleasure with such exquisite care that genuine tears rolled from her eyes when he finally pushed into her. As before dinner earlier, he didn't bother with a condom and it took on new significance. Real marriages—ones with no divorce on the horizon—didn't require condoms.

Was this his way of communicating with her? Of proclaiming his feelings about her and their marriage?

Afterward, he spooned her against him, murmured her

name and he fell asleep as she stroked his leg. And that was when she realized she didn't have a choice. She loved Jason Lynhurst and wanted to be his wife forever. All of the confusion over her feelings and the job offers and everything else blew away.

She loved him. Nothing else mattered. Except for the fact that she still had to figure out how to tell him.

In only a matter of days, Meredith had taken over Jason's condo.

It was the only phrase for it. She had almost no stuff. Basically just the clothes she'd packed from home and the new wardrobe he'd given her. But a simple pair of stilettos in his living room felt more invasive than a military coup.

Her perfume lingered in the air, even after she left.

Their relationship had evolved into something he didn't understand. Somehow. It didn't seem to matter that he'd been trying to keep to the status quo; Meredith did her own thing. The shoes proved the point and he didn't like it.

The front door opened, startling him out of his dead stare at her sandals on the floor.

And there she was in the entry of his condo, hair wild and windblown around her shoulders and a bag of groceries in the crook of one elbow. His heart lurched, a live thing attempting to break free. How had he gotten to the point where simply gazing at Meredith caused all these *things* to happen inside?

"Hey," she called. "I thought you were going to the office."

"It's Saturday," he reminded her needlessly, since they'd had a conversation about that very fact forty-five minutes ago as she'd sailed out the door to pick up a few things. "And you left your shoes in the living room again."

This was the kind of stuff he'd imagined going over with Meiling and reaching a civil agreement about how their life would go. The less change, the better. Meredith ignored him when he tried to explain that the vanity wasn't a catchall for her cosmetics. Actually, that conversation hadn't even made it past the opening argument because she'd dropped her towel with a provocative arch of her eyebrow.

"So?"

Meredith swished into the black granite and stainless-steel kitchen that he'd have sworn was masculine two weeks ago. With his wife in it, the sharp angles softened and the hard glass took on a feminine sheen he'd never noticed before. It was like everything else in the condo; Meredith changed whatever she touched, looked at, breathed on.

Including him. He couldn't keep letting that happen or he'd wake up one day and realize he'd turned into his father overnight. "Someone might trip over them."

She shot him a look over her shoulder as she put some kind of wrapped meat in the refrigerator. "Like the elves that come in during the night?"

He bit back a smile. He didn't want to laugh. This was serious.

"Yeah, that's what I was thinking about. The elven OSHA union," he shot back before he could stop himself.

She giggled and the sound washed over him. He loved her laugh. The condo had been hushed and quiet before she moved in. He'd assumed that was best. Now he wasn't so sure.

Before he could move, she flowed into the living room and climbed into his lap, straddling him like she'd done in the car and his pulse scattered. This was his favorite position, his favorite way to watch her, his favorite way to lose himself in her.

"You should probably punish me, then," she murmured and her hands slipped under his shirt to drive him insane with her touch.

"Meredith." Somehow he had the presence of mind to grab her hands and drag them away from his skin. And then he forgot why he'd been so certain he needed her to stop.

"Yeah, baby?" Then she twisted and crossed her arms behind her back, taking his with them. Her breasts were flush against his chest, exciting them both if the hardness of her nipples was any indication, and his arms were holding her captive. With her mouth inches apart from his, her energy and vibrancy spilled down his throat, and all he could think about was kissing her.

"So is this how it's going to be from now on?" he muttered and sucked in a breath as she shifted deeper into his lap. "I try to have a serious conversation and you distract me with sex?"

"Only if you're saying the shoes are serious." She fluttered her lashes. "Otherwise, I'm just angling for sex. No distraction involved."

Something about her cavalier attitude or the shoes or the swirling mass of uncertainty in the pit of his stomach over the state of their marriage triggered his temper. "Maybe we should have a conversation once in a while."

She hummed happily in her throat. "Mmm. That's my favorite. Talking *and* sex at the same time."

Her hands slipped from his grip and snaked back under his shirt.

He groaned. "That's not what I meant. The merger is at a critical stage. You've got Avery's job offer to consider. We're both at the cusp of our plans coming to fruition and we can't afford to make any missteps."

Saucily, she cocked her head and smiled. "Sounds like a reason to celebrate naked to me."

Then she wiggled expertly against his groin, and nuzzled his neck, working her way up to his lips, where she sucked him into a hot kiss.

He almost lost his train of thought as her tongue found his and deepened the kiss. This couldn't go on. He wrenched away, while his body screamed to dive back in.

"Is sex all you think about?" Frustrated, he pulled her

hands out of his clothes again. He couldn't think when he got wrapped up in her seductive web.

Clueing in finally, she drew back to scowl at him. "No, sugar. Sometimes I do quadratic equations in my head when you're inside me. What would you like me to be thinking about when you're kissing me?"

"I'm sorry." He blew out a breath and tilted his head to touch his forehead to hers. "I'm on edge."

"It's okay." She threaded her fingers through his hair, but instead of turning him volcanic instantly, she caressed him with unveiled tenderness and it split something open inside him. "I'm here for whatever you've got in mind. It doesn't have to be sex."

He shrugged and spit out the first thing he could think of to divert attention from the affectionate moment. "Seems to be the only thing we're good at. Which I guess is appropriate for a relationship based on sex."

Her fingers found his chin and lifted his gaze to hers. Her expression blazed with denial and anger and something else he couldn't begin to understand.

"That's a crock and you know it. We're not just screwing each other. We have an amazing connection and don't you dare devalue what's going on here."

Taken aback at her forcefulness, he stared at her for a moment. "What's going on here?"

She thumped him lightly on the head. "I'm in love with you, you big dolt. Why else would I put up with your horrible sister and your bad attitude and obvious lack of reverence for Jimmy Choos?"

"You're in love with me?" His pulse kicked up, rushing blood from his head. "You can't be."

Shaking her head, she frowned. "Don't tell me how to feel. And I guess that answers my question about whether you feel the same."

No, it didn't. Not at *all*. Because she hadn't asked that and thank God she hadn't because then he'd have to tell her the truth, which was that he didn't know, didn't want to think about it. "Our marriage is advantageous. Period."

True statement. Or at least it used to be. Somewhere along the way, things had changed. And he didn't like that, either. She'd mixed up his plans with her unwanted declarations and sweet personality and amazing insight into… everything.

"Jason." She paused, her chest heaving. "Being in love has far more advantages than your 'marriage is a tool' spiel."

"Not for me," he countered. "Love destroyed everything I've ever worked for. I don't believe in it. Don't believe it can last, don't believe someone can make a lifelong decision so quickly about whether a person will stick with you forever."

That went for both of them—how could she possibly trust him with her heart after all of this? He wasn't a good bet for a relationship.

Disappointment pulled at her mouth. "Nothing that's happened in the last couple of weeks challenges that?"

Everything that had happened in the past couple of weeks challenged him. He'd tried avoiding it, tried keeping things on an even keel, bargained, flung out off-the-cuff counteroffers. None of it had worked to keep this woman out of his arms or out of his heart.

And it kind of made him wonder whether that had actually been his goal. "I've never made a secret out of what I hoped to achieve from this marriage."

"Well, guess what? Sometimes you don't get what you pay for. And sometimes you do," she countered cryptically. "Do you want to know what I wanted to get out of this marriage?"

"A divorce. You've been very clear."

And he'd done everything in his power to stop that from happening. He didn't want to let her go and he pretended it was about the merger, when in reality, it was about avoiding what was happening between them so he didn't have to face his shortcomings. If this marriage morphed into a love affair, he'd have to be a better, different man than his father. What if he couldn't do it?

"No. I hoped to find out who I'm going to be when I grow up."

The memory blazed through him instantly—that first night together, in his hotel room. After she'd turned his world into a wicked den of hedonistic pleasure, they'd lain draped across his bed. The scent of her perfume had emanated from his sheets and lingered on his skin. She'd pillowed her head on his stomach, gloriously, unashamedly naked, and told him being a grown-up scared her because she didn't know who she was going to be.

But that had been two years ago.

Puzzled at her deliberate reference to Las Vegas, he asked, "That was what the Grown-Up Pact was about. Don't you already know?"

"I didn't. Not for a long time. But I finally figured it out." She contemplated him for a long moment. "I'm curious about something. You cooked up this plan to fix the broken company in Vegas, right?" When he nodded, she continued. "Say you become the CEO like you've envisioned and you start your merger plans. Voilà! Lynhurst Enterprises is reunited. Then what?"

What did this have to do with what she wanted to be when she grew up? "What do you mean, then what? Everything will be like it was."

"What's so great about that? Did the two halves complement each other? Have they struggled apart? What are you going to do with the reunited halves to prove to everyone that you had the right idea all along?"

Speechless, he stared at her. Because he had no answer. He and Avery had talked about launching a new line, but the intent was to drum up buzz and goodwill for the newly formed company. Past that, he'd done nothing to strategize or determine the best path forward.

Because he'd been too busy strategizing how to best use his marriage to keep Meredith in his arms. She'd messed him up more than he'd realized.

Her smile softened his shock. "See? You haven't figured it out, either. These are the same kinds of questions you asked me about why wedding dresses and it helped me think through what I'm doing with my life. We need each other. I love you, but I have no idea how to be married. No idea what it means for either of us or the dreams we've talked about. Let's figure out what being a grown-up means. Together. Don't walk away this time."

There was that word again. *Love.* It was no longer a nebulous concept he'd grown to hate because it had been Paul's excuse for all his selfish moves two years ago. But what was it, if not that?

Confusion kicked up his temper, burning at the base of his throat. Everything had come to a head in an instant. There was no more leverage, no more excuses, just a woman freely offering her love. What if he accepted it? Would he be like his father, eventually sacrificing the good of Lynhurst Enterprises for his wife?

But how did he know what would be good for Lynhurst Enterprises? He couldn't even answer a simple question about his post-merger plans, and his track record for earning a promotion to CEO started and ended with accidentally marrying a woman his mother approved of.

Which he'd then turned around and used as leverage to keep Meredith around. It was far worse than anything Avery had done in the pursuit of winning. A sick sense of dread heated his chest.

He couldn't think with Meredith in his lap. Carefully, he set her on the couch and turned away, unable to look at her for fear she'd read something in his expression he didn't want to reveal.

"I can't—" He swallowed. He couldn't even say it.

He didn't deserve her. She didn't deserve to be married to him, a manipulative SOB who'd suddenly realized he didn't want to be handed anything because of how he'd spun the situation. They weren't even married because he'd earned Meredith's love. It was an accident.

She was right. He hadn't figured out how to grow up in Vegas.

"Why can't we go back to the way things were?" he asked, desperation pulling things out of his mouth without his consent. "Why does love have to be a part of this?"

But it was too late to go back. He knew that. Two years too late.

"Because that's what I want," she suggested quietly. "I won't settle for less than everything. I spent two years trying to forget you and it didn't work. Because I fell in love with you in Vegas and was too stupid to realize it. I want what we started back then."

"Vegas wasn't real."

It had been a mirage, guiding him down the wrong path. Guiding him toward a goal he could never achieve. The broken company wasn't going to magically come back together because he'd written a few documents describing the new corporate structure. Even if he and Avery pulled off the merger, it wouldn't magically fix all the problems he had with his sister or with his father, both of whom he would be working with again.

And he'd become CEO because he'd gotten *married*. Not because he'd created a vision for the company's future. Not because he'd earned it.

If Vegas wasn't real, then neither was anything in his relationship with Meredith.

"Yes. It was real," she insisted. "As real as what's happening in our marriage. Can't you see that what happened in Vegas wasn't ever meant to stay there?"

"Vegas was about sex," he said flatly. "You can't sit

there and tell me you were waxing philosophical when you were screaming my name that second time in the shower."

Harsh. But he needed to distance her. For once. He didn't trust himself one iota at this point.

Coolly, she blinked. "But afterward, I didn't get dressed and leave. I'm glad I didn't because that's when we connected. It may have started out as two people with a mutual need for an anonymous release, but that's not how it ended. The whole time, we were taking baby steps toward the future, but it's a future where we're together forever. That's the point. It still hasn't ended because neither of us wants it to end."

As always, she read him easily. "You're right. I could have ended this many times and I didn't."

Because he was incredibly selfish. *That* was how he was like his father, a danger he'd ignored, assuming love was the problem when all along it was something else entirely. Something he had no idea how to guard against.

He'd been turning their relationship to his advantage from second one, ensuring he alone had all the leverage and peeking under every rock to uncover her motives so she didn't get the drop on him.

The whole time he'd been wondering what she was doing to him, it never occurred to him to pay attention to what he was doing to her. He'd been leading her to expectationville by inviting her into his home, and into his bed.

He owed it to her to give her the divorce she'd come for so she could get started on being a grown-up. Without him there to screw it up for her again.

"We can't have a real marriage and I can't be in love with you," he told her dully.

Not yet. Maybe not ever, but he couldn't ask her to stick around until he learned to be selfless. He owed her for everything she'd done for him. Letting her go was the right thing. The grown-up thing.

The stark emotion in her expression clawed at his windpipe and he shut his eyes for a beat. When he opened them, tears had gathered in her eyes and she shook her head in disbelief.

"That's it? You're giving up what we have?"

"I have to." Let her interpret that in whatever way she chose. "I'll sign the papers. It's the least I can do."

She stood and locked her knees. "This is your chance to have everything, to take what you want, like you did two years ago, like you do every time we're together. Stop letting your head rule your heart."

Mute, he stared at her, unable to conceive of anything else he could say that would make a difference. Besides, he was afraid if he started talking, the truth would pour out. That he'd like nothing better than to do exactly as she suggested and chuck it all in favor of a blistering love affair with his wife.

But he couldn't. She deserved a grown-up husband.

Nodding, she firmed her mouth. "I'll be out of the loft by five."

"You're leaving?" *What else would she do, moron?* It hadn't quite hit him that he was letting her go forever until that moment.

"Yeah. Me and my broken heart will go somewhere you're not, but this time, I won't come back." She reached into her purse and pulled out a slip of paper, then scribbled something on it. "Send the divorce papers to this address."

He glanced at it. *Houston.* So she was going home. That was best for her. "For what it's worth, I'm sorry it had to end this way."

She nodded and fled to the bedroom.

He got his bag and went to the office after all, without saying goodbye. There was no way he could watch her pack.

Once at his desk, he didn't turn on his laptop. Instead, he rested his aching head on the cool cover and wondered if Meredith even realized he'd sacrificed his CEO position and put the merger in jeopardy by giving her the divorce she no longer wanted.

If she went home, Avery would lose Allo for sure, and Hurst would crumble. No one on Lyn's executive team would approve a merger with a failing company. And Bettina would yank back her support for his promotion without a wife by his side.

And the only part he cared about was that he'd hurt Meredith, which he would never forgive himself for. Somehow, he had to find a way to make it up to her.

Thirteen

The white sand of Barbados stretched out as far as the eye could see and a balmy breeze played with Meredith's hair. The sun shone, she was relaxing in a bikini and the resort hadn't opened yet, so it wasn't crowded. Paradise—except for the part where she was miserable.

She'd walked away from Jason again, but this time, he'd kicked her out the door. It was over and she'd lost the only man she'd ever loved. Probably the only man she ever *would* love.

And with absolutely no emotion on his face, he'd stared her dead in the eye and chosen divorce instead of love. It was a flat-out declaration of the temperature of his blood—cold. Obviously she was as empty-headed as she'd always feared if she hadn't seen that coming.

Meredith sucked the bottom out of her piña colada and wished it had deadened even a tenth of the pain a shattered heart caused. If the past two years were any indication, she had a long, difficult ride ahead full of painful memories.

Her sister, Cara, who was stretched out in the next lounge chair sewing the bodice piece of what would become some bride's happily-ever-after dress, glanced at Meredith's glass longingly. "Can you drink another one and let me watch?"

"Alcohol envy?" Meredith suggested with raised brows. When Meredith had shown up in Barbados without call-

ing and without explanation, Cara had simply hugged her
and said she was so glad to see her. Because she hadn't
wanted to tell Meredith over the phone that she was pregnant.

Everything else ceased to matter in that moment as Meredith had smiled and laughed with her sister over the joyous
news. Cara had survived an emotionally painful miscar-
riage with her first pregnancy and Meredith prayed this
time it would stick.

"And how." Cara patted her bare stomach. "I won't be
able to drink for like another year and a half because I'm
planning to breastfeed."

That was enough to start the tears again. Why, Meredith had no clue. It wasn't as if she'd gotten to the point
of thinking about having Jason's baby. She wasn't mother
material—at least not yet. But it was hard to be around
someone so blissfully happy, who'd figured out how to
navigate choppy relationship waters.

It was a skill and Meredith lacked it. Obviously.

"Honey, that's the third time." Cara rubbed her shoulder. "Maybe one of these days you'll tell me what happened in New York?"

Meredith had arrived in Barbados a week and a half ago
and somehow, after the baby news and diving right into
being Cara's assistant again and the slightly numb feeling
that never eased, well…talking about Jason had gone from
hard to impossible.

"Guy trouble," she mumbled and adjusted the strap on
her bikini.

God Almighty, what else could she possibly say? *I went
to New York for a divorce, fell in love with my husband
all over again and got dumped like yesterday's trash. Oh,
that's right, you didn't know I got married. See, there was
this trip to Vegas…*

Cara rolled her eyes. "Duh. I've just never seen you cry

over a guy before. Find another one. You've always got some man on a string."

"You say that like it's a bad thing," Meredith sniffed. "And I've tried finding another one. It's useless."

"Honey, you've only been here less than two weeks. Give it time."

"I've been trying for two years," Meredith muttered under her breath.

Plus three weeks, which was how long ago she'd left New York, broken and bleeding and too proud to admit to anyone what a mess she'd made of her life because she was flat dumb enough to think an accidental marriage to a man she'd met in *Las Vegas* would work out.

Cara, cheer-up speech in full swing, waved the needle in her fingers at the interior of the resort beyond the beach. "Find another pool boy, like Paolo, and let him talk your clothes off. Paolo seemed pretty good at making you smile."

Meredith searched her memory. "Paolo? Oh, from the Grace Bay resort."

She and Cara had attended a bridal expo in Turks and Caicos last fall, where Cara had reconnected with Keith, the man responsible for her current blissful condition. Meredith had chased yet another set of gorgeous abs while trying to forget Jason.

"I was faking it," she informed her sister. "Paolo is obviously very forgettable."

"Obviously." Cara fell silent for a moment and then cocked her head. "Can you at least tell me if you're planning to stay? Because if you're going home, I have a couple of things lined up for you to take care of. You know, if you're still interested in being partners."

It was the perfect segue into a difficult subject, but it was one Meredith needed to address. That was what grown-ups did—tell people the truth, even when it was hard. "I have to be honest. I'm not sure what I want to do, but I know that wedding dresses is your dream, not mine. Would you hate me forever if I backed out?"

Meredith wasn't willing to settle for a job unless she could be passionate about it, and it wasn't fair to Cara for Meredith to go into a partnership unless she could give her whole heart.

With a smile, Cara shook her head. "Not at all. I was hoping you'd eventually figure out that it wasn't what you really wanted. But I would have welcomed you regardless."

How had she gotten lucky enough to be related to such a wise woman?

Cara stretched and motioned at the dress she'd been stitching. "I'm at a stopping place and I need to get out of the sun."

Meredith nodded and helped her sister carry her sewing supplies so she wouldn't get sand in the dress pieces. They walked through the pool area to the main building and not one pool boy caught Meredith's eye.

The mention of Grace Bay also reminded her that Cara had walked a similar path as Meredith. Albeit much more successfully, as she was currently carrying the baby of the man she'd married, despite a rocky beginning to their relationship, which had included Keith leaving Cara at the altar the first time they'd planned to get married.

"You and Keith got back together after two years. How did you make it work the second time around?"

Cara shrugged and paused at the front desk to situate the fabric over her arm. "We didn't know each other well the first time. When I ran into him again in Grace Bay, I swore I wasn't falling for him again. But I was so jealous of you and how easily you seemed to love 'em and leave 'em. I wanted to try that. Keith was supposed to be my tropical island fling. I clearly missed the memo about how a fling works."

Her sister laughed as Meredith shook her head. "I'm the last person you should be jealous of. I suck at everything."

"The only thing you suck at, sweetheart, is paperwork."

The familiar masculine voice washed over her as she and Cara jerked their heads simultaneously to view the speaker.

And there stood the man of her fantasies, in the flesh. Jason—with one hand stuck in his khaki pants pocket and an intense smile deepening his delicious cheekbones.

He'd come for her. He missed her. He was sorry and wanted to try again.

"Jason," Meredith croaked. "What—"

"Well, *hello* there," Cara interrupted with an inquisitive brow lift and an extended hand, dress pieces forgotten on the front desk. "Cara Mitchell. You must be the reason my sister is visiting me in Barbados?"

"Yeah, seems like." Jason held out his hand to shake Cara's. "Jason Lynhurst. Meredith's husband."

Crap. That had *not* just come out of his mouth. That was so like a man. As if he could fly in here and she'd fall into his arms, as if everything was fine and they were a married couple meeting in Barbados, as planned. All is forgiven. *Let's get it on, little wife.* Jerk.

"Oh, my." Cara tsked as she barged on past Meredith's squeak of denial. "This is a far better story than I was hoping. Do tell."

Meredith unstuck her tongue from the roof of her mouth and elbowed her sister in the ribs. "I'm standing right here."

"Uh-huh," Cara agreed. "And yet you've never breathed the word 'husband' to me one single time, so maybe you should hush up and let me talk to my brother-in-law."

"As if." Meredith tossed her head and zeroed in on Jason with equal parts attitude and scorn. Just to cover the nervous flutter of her pulse at the sight of his gorgeous self not three feet from her. "You shouldn't go around sneaking up on people who deliberately flew thousands of miles away to hide. And you definitely shouldn't introduce yourself as my husband."

"Then you definitely shouldn't have married me," he countered brightly.

Too brightly, especially for a man who—if life was fair—was miserable without her and had tracked her down in the Caribbean because he wanted to throw himself at her feet, begging for mercy.

She might even forgive him after a fair amount of groveling. Or she might not. Too early to tell.

That's when she noticed the manila folder in his hand, like the kind used to hold important papers. Her pulse dropped. He'd tracked her down all right. To finally divorce her, once and for all.

Her stupidity knew no bounds.

"What are you doing here?" She crossed her arms before he noticed her shaking hands. "You were supposed to mail me the divorce papers, not deliver them personally."

"I did mail them. Three weeks ago. But funny thing—I never got my copy of the filed papers back."

Neither of them broke the staring contest they had going on as Cara murmured that she had something else to do and slipped away.

"I didn't get the papers." Because she'd gotten on a plane to Barbados, too numb to even think of mentioning to her mother that she was expecting divorce papers in the mail. Guess she'd proven beyond a shadow of a doubt that she couldn't be trusted to resolve adult problems like filing for a divorce.

She glared at him. "If you came here to rub it in how much of a dingbat I am about paperwork, you're two years too late."

His expression softened. "I'm here because I finally figured out what I want to be when I grow up. But I can't do it without you."

The words lanced through her. Why would he deliberately throw that into the mix now, when she'd already tried to have this conversation back in New York? It was too little, too late.

"You want to be CEO," Meredith reminded him. "You made it really clear you don't need me for that."

She'd laid everything on the line: her heart, her future, her happiness, her marriage. Even her job prospects. All with the belief that he'd been warming up to the possibility of forever, only to be crushed with the truth. He wasn't willing to give her the one thing she wanted from their marriage—love.

"Maybe this will help explain." He handed her the folder. "Go ahead. Read it."

The manila folder scalded her hand and she nearly dropped it. "I know what the divorce papers say. My father's lawyer drew them up."

With an intense once-over she didn't dare interpret, he shook his head. "It's not what you think. Inside is the manifesto for revamping Lynhurst Enterprises. Bettina, Paul, Avery and I worked on it together."

Meredith's eyes narrowed even as her fingers curled around the folder, itching to open it and verify what he was telling her. "The four of you were in the same room? And no homicide detectives had to be called?"

His smile melted her and she forgot to breathe. Apparently her body hadn't gotten the message that this man wasn't hers anymore.

"It was touch and go for the first couple of meetings. But I remembered what we talked about. How Lynhurst Enterprises is my passion and I'd sacrifice anything for it because it was built by people with my blood. Figured it was time to put it to the test."

A little off balance, she opened the folder. Page after page of black type detailed a mind-numbingly comprehensive business plan. Like he'd said. "I don't understand. What happened to the merger plans you worked on with Avery?"

Jason's need for vengeance against his father couldn't have vanished so easily. Neither could his rivalry with Avery. They'd both been his sole focus for too long.

"Some of it is still in there, but it's better now. The manifesto details the restructuring of Lyn and Hurst under one umbrella using Hurst's capital and incorporating Lyn's soul." He reached for her hand and held it to his heart, a bold move that she appreciated enough to keep from snatching her hand back. "It's nearly complete, but it's missing one important stamp of approval. Yours. The only Lynhurst who hasn't reviewed it yet."

"Um…what?" Meredith's cheeks went hot at the same moment her spine went cold. "You want me to be involved in this? Why? I'm not a Lynhurst."

But she wanted to be and for more reasons than solely to be Jason's wife. She'd found a place in the world where she truly fit, where her mind mattered far more than her body and he'd ripped it away from her.

Only to appear out of thin air and offer her…what?

His gaze grew heavy with significance and she couldn't look away.

"You were the inspiration for the whole thing, Meredith. Avery quoted you. Bettina quoted you. I don't think I had an original thought the entire time. It was all you. We used everything the marketing department came up with to refute Avery's sweatshop allegations and it all took off from there." He gripped her hand tighter. "You are a Lynhurst. At heart, where it's most important. It's one of the many things I learned from you. Leading with my heart is not easy for me and I needed to get better at it. Unfortunately, it came at a terrible price—it cost me you."

Her eyes burned as she registered the sweet vulnerability in his gaze, the same way he looked at her when they were connecting. That nearly undid her. "It didn't have to cost anything. I loved you for free."

It was a vicious reminder that she didn't want his money,

or his loft, or a job offer from anyone named Lynhurst. Just Jason's love, and he'd handed her heart back to her. She didn't know if she could trust him with it again.

I loved you. Past tense. *God, please don't let me be too late.*

When Jason had left New York for Houston, he'd hoped she hadn't filed the papers yet because she didn't want to. Because she wanted to try again, like he did. Never had it crossed his mind that he'd get to Houston and discover his wife had fled to the Caribbean. And that he'd have to scrap his entire rehearsed speech since he had no idea *what* her state of mind would be when he found her.

Jason swallowed the lump in his throat and flexed the muscles in his hand, which ached to pull Meredith into his embrace.

But her steely expression hadn't given an inch since he'd started talking and she wouldn't welcome him with open arms. Not yet. But maybe soon, if he could somehow explain the decisions he'd made, and the path he'd forced himself to walk the past few weeks. He'd let her storm out of his life, convinced she would be better off without him, only to discover that he yearned to be the man she deserved…and worked tirelessly fourteen hours a day until he felt closer to it than he ever had before.

Now he needed to know if she agreed that he'd become worthy of her.

"You gave me your heart freely, Meredith." Greedily, he searched her face for some sign she still had those feelings, but her guarded expression gave him few clues. "But I hadn't done anything to earn your love. Letting you go was the hardest thing I've ever done. I didn't want to."

Growing up sucked. But if Meredith forgave him for taking so long to figure out what that looked like, it would all be worth it. Assuming she didn't tell him to take a hike, which she would be well within her rights to do.

"Why *did* you let me go, then?" Meredith demanded. "I would have stayed and worked through the manifesto with you. I would have helped you figure out how to lead with your heart. I wanted to."

"I know." God, did he ever. The look on her face when he'd told her he couldn't love her…awake or asleep, it had haunted him. "I'm sorry, honey. So sorry that I hurt you, but I wasn't good enough for you. Hell, I couldn't even give you what you needed. What did I know about love? Staying wouldn't have worked. Or been fair to you."

The shadows in her eyes didn't magically fade. "So you sent me away for my own good. Forgive me for not thanking you. You did it so you could focus on Lynhurst Enterprises. That's always been more important than me."

The hurt in her voice cut through him and he cursed under his breath. He was screwing this up, which was what happened when you went into a potentially volatile situation with no plan and no backup. But he'd come unprepared on purpose, carrying with him the only thing he could possibly offer—his love.

He'd hoped it would be enough.

"Sweetheart, my plans for Lynhurst Enterprises are over. That's what the manifesto is all about. I needed to grow up and you helped me not only see that, but do it. You were my inspiration for walking into that room full of Lynhursts with the intent of working together on a common goal. And I did it because nothing is more important to me than you."

With her at the top of the list—even above Lynhurst Enterprises—his vision cleared and allowed him to see what needed to happen with the company in a way he'd never have imagined. Who would have thought that falling in love would actually make him a better executive?

"What are you saying?" she whispered. "That you want to try again?"

She was killing him. This was the most painful conversation he'd ever had, but he wouldn't get better at being honest with his feelings by keeping them to himself. Or by hiding behind a ridiculous marriage philosophy that only facilitated selfishness.

"There's no trying this time." He flipped open the folder again and pulled out the divorce papers, which he'd tucked behind the manifesto. "Only choices. Here's the signed divorce decree. If you want to file it, file it. I hope you don't because that's not what I want. But it's your choice to make."

His pulse raced with uncertainty and genuine fear at giving up his edge with Meredith, but he'd left New York bent on ensuring she knew exactly what she meant to him.

Standing before her wasn't good enough. He sank to one knee, still clutching her hand like a lifeline. Because in many ways, she was. She'd breathed life into his cold heart and he couldn't imagine it beating properly without her.

"Meredith, I love you. No leverage. No deal. I never want you to question if I'm married to you because it's advantageous. I'm choosing to be with you because I love you. Choose to be with me because you love me, too. No other reason."

Stricken, she stared down at him. "What about trouncing Avery for the CEO position? Did you just hand it to her? Tell me you didn't do that."

His heart went heavy. Of course she'd ask about that. What had he done to convince her he truly didn't care who won?

"Page fifteen," he told her softly. The verbiage was etched on his soul since he was the one who'd written the clause. "Paul will assume the CEO's office until he retires, at which point the job will go to whomever the executive committee appoints." He shrugged, his pulse pounding in his throat. "That's the fairest way, right? If I earn the job, great. If not, I'll keep being the best COO I can."

And he'd be working for his father. A reality Jason couldn't have possibly envisioned without Meredith in his life. He needed her to keep him sane after a long day in the fashion-world trenches.

She didn't open the folder or even glance at it. "If you're not going to be CEO when you grow up, who are you going to be?"

"I want to be your husband." The phrase scratched at the back of his throat, and of all things, his eyes burned a little, too. "If you'll have me. I love you so much and I'm sorry it took me so long to become the man I should have been when you married me."

In a tangle of long hair and bikini and killer body, she launched into his arms, holding him as if she never wanted to let go. Which worked for him. His heart filled so fast, it was a wonder it didn't burst like a dropped watermelon.

"Is that a—"

"Yes," she finished for him. "It's a yes."

His smile was so wide, his cheeks hurt. "I love it when you finish my sentences."

That should have been his first clue they were made for each other. He'd lost track of the number of times they'd completed each other's thoughts. It was a natural progression to completing each other's lives.

"I love it when you chase after me."

Unable to stop touching her, he smoothed her hair back from her face. "So tell me. Who do you want to be when you grow up?"

She shot him an enigmatic smile and kicked the folder full of paperwork across the floor. "Mrs. Lynhurst."

The title blasted through him with a thrill. And a punch of agony. If only they'd gotten the answers to these questions right two years ago, they might have walked away from that weekend in Vegas with a totally different life. Because at the end of the day, Vegas wasn't about coming up with a plan for growing up. It was about finding someone worth growing up for.

"No divorce, then?" he asked, his heart aching in anticipation of the answer.

"I'm shredding the papers," she said decisively. "Isn't that what you do with something you don't want to fall into the wrong hands?"

Her gaze skittered down his body and left a whole lot of heat in its wake. "Yep. Credit card numbers, legal documents. Divorce decrees that you realize you never should have agreed to sign in the first place."

Someone cleared their throat and Jason glanced up to see Meredith's sister holding the hand of a dark-haired man with a look of authority about him.

The resort wasn't open to guests yet, as it was apparently undergoing some type of renovation. Meredith's name had gotten him past the front gate, but beyond finding his wife and settling their future, he hadn't thought about anyone witnessing his near-disastrous makeup session.

Jason climbed to his feet and pulled Meredith to hers.

The dark-haired man leaned forward to clasp Jason's hand. "Keith Mitchell. I've been waiting a long time to shake your hand."

With a small laugh, Jason shook his head. "I just got here."

"Yeah, but I've been dying to meet the man with the fortitude to fall in love with Meredith for ages. You bring your steel-plated armor?"

Meredith glared at her brother-in-law. "Shut it, Mitchell."

Jason grinned. "It's in my other suitcase."

It was a far different family dynamic than the one he was used to, but he liked it.

Keith nodded. "Good man. If you have any problems during your stay, you let me know so I can address them."

"Are we staying?" he asked Meredith.

"Uh, yeah. Unless you had another honeymoon getaway planned? You know, to make up for not taking me on one the first time." The sizzling once-over she treated him to said she'd like to get him behind locked doors quickly.

And he'd like to let her. He'd missed her fiercely.

"Some people would consider a weekend in Vegas a honeymoon," he suggested without an ounce of irony.

"And some people actually propose to their wives. With like a ring and everything." Her arched brow made him laugh. "It's a good thing for you that I'm the soul of forgiveness."

Yes, it was a good thing for him. Otherwise, he'd be going back to New York without her and living the rest of his life in misery.

Cara snapped her fingers. "Lynhurst! Of course. That's why you look so familiar." She glared at Meredith. "I can forgive you for getting married and not telling me, but marrying Bettina Lynhurst's son and failing to mention it is plain cruel."

With a sigh, Meredith waved at Jason. "Cara, meet the heir to the Lynhurst couture empire, also known as the man I can't seem to get rid of no matter how many times I ask for a divorce."

Cara glanced between the two of them as if she was watching a fascinating tennis match. "Really? How many times have you asked?"

"Too many," Meredith muttered, as Jason said, "Never. She mostly orders me to sign the papers. Except when she's asking me not to."

"Geez, this is better than a soap opera," Cara said. "How long have you been married?"

"Two years," Meredith admitted.

"But only because we didn't know," Jason added. "Meredith kindly informed me when she came to New York and changed my entire life."

Two years ago, he'd been wandering around looking for a plan, an idea—*something*—to make him feel whole. And he'd found it. By some miracle, she'd fallen in love with him and done it all over again. Meredith had turned him into a man he could be proud of.

"I don't get it," Keith interjected with a furrowed brow. "How did you get married two years ago?"

Jason glanced at Meredith to gauge whether or not she wanted to keep that a secret. But she nodded with a sigh. "Seems like the whole story is bound to come out anyway."

"Equal parts Las Vegas, tequila shots and an Elvis impersonator." Jason caught Meredith's hand and brought it to his lips. "Best mistake I've ever made."

Fingers over her mouth, Cara half laughed and half gasped. "You didn't."

"It wasn't supposed to be real," Meredith insisted. "We never intended for the papers to be filed. Somehow I messed up and here we are, thanks to my boneheaded mistake."

She shot him a smile that warmed him thoroughly. "Luckily, you were boneheaded enough to fall in love with me, too."

And then his wife kissed him.

Epilogue

Meredith pushed open the door of the loft she shared with her husband, humming happily despite a ten-hour day that had included Allo dropping a bolt of fabric on her foot, Avery herding her into a two-hour marketing meeting and Jason not responding to the sexy text message she'd sent on the way home.

It was all good when you lived in the most exciting city in the world with a supportive husband who loved you.

Both Jason and Bettina had begged her to take jobs working for them at Lyn, but she turned them both down to go back to work for Allo. Maybe it was crazy, but Meredith wanted to prove she could make it in New York on her own terms.

Said supportive husband had beaten her home and she took a long minute to soak in the visual splendor waiting for her in the living room. The view of the New York skyline wasn't bad, either, but it couldn't hold a candle to the gorgeous man lounging on the couch, wearing a mischievous smile.

"About time you got home," Jason scolded without any heat. "I've been waiting very patiently."

Eyebrows raised, she surveyed the bottle of golden liquor and two shot glasses spread out on the coffee table. "Trying to get me drunk so you can take advantage of me? Because you know good and well you don't need alcohol for that."

"Figured you needed a break after working all day with the most horrible boss in the world."

Meredith grinned and climbed into Jason's lap—astride, her favorite way to talk to him. "But tequila shots?"

"For our anniversary." Settling his hands in place against her waist, he nestled her closer. "That's what we did on our wedding night. Figured we should keep the tradition."

It wasn't their anniversary. That wouldn't happen for another couple of months, but the thought was sweet. So sweet, she felt compelled to blurt out, "I have a confession. I didn't actually drink the shots in Vegas."

She'd poured them out when Jason wasn't looking, mostly because she didn't want to hurt his feelings, but also because tequila was vile.

"Um…neither did I. I don't like tequila straight." His blue eyes bored into hers as they shared a long glance heavy with dawning comprehension.

"So wait. How many drinks had actually made it down your throat when you came up with the brilliant idea to find the all-night wedding chapel?"

Guilt clouded Jason's expression. "Maybe two."

Figured. Meredith dissolved into a fit of giggles. "Guess we can't tell people we got drunk and got married anymore. What'll we say instead?"

Jason's chuckle warmed her from the inside out. "The truth. That we fell in love and got married but were too worried about what other people would think to claim our happiness."

"Whew. Glad we're not that young and stupid any longer."

He grinned. "What are we going to do to celebrate now that we've established we both hate tequila?"

"Guess we'll have to do something we both like." Shooting him a sultry smile, she plunked the remote into her hand. "Watch *Project Runway*."

With a growl, he knocked the remote to the carpet and

treated her to a scorching-hot kiss that communicated every bit of his love and desire for her. Who needed fashion on television when she'd already found the perfect fit?

* * * * *

If you loved Meredith's romance,
pick up her sister, Cara's, story:

FROM EX TO ETERNITY

Available now from award-winning
author Kat Cantrell and Harlequin Desire!

If you're on Twitter, tell us what you think of
Harlequin Desire! #harlequindesire

REQUEST YOUR FREE BOOKS!
2 FREE NOVELS PLUS 2 FREE GIFTS!

HARLEQUIN *Desire*

ALWAYS POWERFUL, PASSIONATE AND PROVOCATIVE

YES! Please send me 2 FREE Harlequin Desire® novels and my 2 FREE gifts (gifts are worth about $10). After receiving them, if I don't wish to receive any more books, I can return the shipping statement marked "cancel." If I don't cancel, I will receive 6 brand-new novels every month and be billed just $4.55 per book in the U.S. or $4.99 per book in Canada. That's a savings of at least 13% off the cover price! It's quite a bargain! Shipping and handling is just 50¢ per book in the U.S. and 75¢ per book in Canada.* I understand that accepting the 2 free books and gifts places me under no obligation to buy anything. I can always return a shipment and cancel at any time. Even if I never buy another book, the two free books and gifts are mine to keep forever.

225/326 HDN F4ZC

Name _____ (PLEASE PRINT)

Address _____ Apt. #

City _____ State/Prov. _____ Zip/Postal Code

Signature (if under 18, a parent or guardian must sign)

Mail to the **Harlequin® Reader Service:**

IN U.S.A.: P.O. Box 1867, Buffalo, NY 14240-1867
IN CANADA: P.O. Box 609, Fort Erie, Ontario L2A 5X3

Want to try two free books from another line?
Call 1-800-873-8635 or visit www.ReaderService.com.

* Terms and prices subject to change without notice. Prices do not include applicable taxes. Sales tax applicable in N.Y. Canadian residents will be charged applicable taxes. Offer not valid in Quebec. This offer is limited to one order per household. Not valid for current subscribers to Harlequin Desire books. All orders subject to credit approval. Credit or debit balances in a customer's account(s) may be offset by any other outstanding balance owed by or to the customer. Please allow 4 to 6 weeks for delivery. Offer available while quantities last.

Your Privacy—The Harlequin® Reader Service is committed to protecting your privacy. Our Privacy Policy is available online at www.ReaderService.com or upon request from the Harlequin Reader Service.

We make a portion of our mailing list available to reputable third parties that offer products we believe may interest you. If you prefer that we not exchange your name with third parties, or if you wish to clarify or modify your communication preferences, please visit us at www.ReaderService.com/consumerschoice or write to us at Harlequin Reader Service Preference Service, P.O. Box 9062, Buffalo, NY 14269. Include your complete name and address.

HD13R

*Alex Ramon is all business when he's tasked with
restoring his country's royal family to the throne.
But when his sexy assistant cozies up to a prince,
his unexpected jealousy requires him to mix work
with pleasure...*

Read on for a sneak peek at
MINDING HER BOSS'S BUSINESS
the passionate first installment in the
DYNASTIES: THE MONTOROS *series!*

When a small orchestra launched into their first song,
Alex stood and held out his hand. "Do you feel like
dancing?"

He knew it was a tactical error as soon as he took
Maria in his arms. Given the situation, he'd assumed
dancing was a socially acceptable way to pass the time.

He was wrong. Dead wrong. No matter the public
venue or the circumspect way in which he held her, nothing could erase the fact that Maria was soft and warm in
his embrace. The slick fabric of her dress did nothing to
disguise the skin beneath.

He found his breath caught in his throat, lodged there
by a sharp stab of hunger. He'd worked so hard these past
weeks he'd let his personal needs slide. Celibacy was
neither smart nor sustainable. Certainly not when faced
daily with such deliciously carnal temptation.

When he couldn't think of a good reason to let her

go, one dance turned into three. Inevitably, his body responded to her nearness.

He was in heaven and hell, shuddering with arousal and unable to do a thing about it.

When the potential future prince brushed past them, his petite sister in his arms, Alex remembered what he had meant to say earlier. "Maria…"

"Hmm?"

Her voice had the warm, honeyed sound of a woman pleasured by her lover. Alex cleared his throat. "You need to be careful around Gabriel Montoro."

Maria's reaction was unmistakable. She went rigid and pulled away. "Excuse me?" Beautiful eyes glared at him.

Alex soldiered on. "He's a mature, experienced man, and you are very young. I'd hate to see him take advantage of you."

Maria went pale but for two spots of hectic color on her cheekbones. "Your concern is duly noted," she said, the words icy. "But you'll have to trust my judgment, I'm afraid."

Find out if Alex heeds Maria's advice (hint: he doesn't!)
in MINDING HER BOSS'S BUSINESS
by USA TODAY bestselling author
Janice Maynard.
Available May 2015 wherever
Harlequin Desire books and ebooks are sold

www.Harlequin.com